"You're naked," Brandi said slowly.

Sebastian looked down at himself in mock surprise. "I guess I took my clothes off to shower. That's usually the way it's done, isn't it?"

She carefully licked her lips, her gaze now glued desperately to his. "You're...awfully big."

Chuckling, he replied, "Hmm. And I'm not nearly so impressive as I *can* be." He'd been relieved to see it was true—he didn't want to scare her off.

She shook her head. "I wasn't talking about that. I meant you are just so massive. All over."

"I know. I was teasing you." *Damn.* He couldn't very well stay unenthusiastic if she continued to stare at him this way. He had to distract himself, so he moved to the sink and grabbed his razor.

As Sebastian went through the familiar motions of shaving, Brandi watched in fascinated silence. He couldn't help himself any longer—his body stirred with her interest. And at the sight she looked absurdly amazed.

He tried to grin, but failed. He had to believe she would be his soon. *Very* soon. Or he'd never survive this vacation.

Dear Reader,

Though not everyone will admit it, we all have fantasies, from the tame to the risqué. Some people get to realize their fantasies, most don't. But for Brandi Sommers, the heroine in my story, sexy Sebastian Sinclair is determined not only to discover her fantasies, but to fulfill them as well. And he does—with great skill and tenderness.

I had so much fun writing this book, not only because I love the characters, but because of the new freedom afforded by BLAZE. I've often been told I push the boundaries, both in theme and with my explicit love scenes. Hallelujah! I want to push. Life is real, love is real...fantasies are real. To write about them without total honesty would be to cheat my characters, and my readers.

I hope you'll enjoy reading *Fantasy* as much as I enjoyed writing it. Let me know what you think. And in the meantime, I hope all *your* fantasies come true.

Lori

P.S. If you'd like to correspond with Lori, please send an SASE to P.O. Box 854, Ross, OH 45061.

It's hot...and it's every woman's secret fantasy....

Don't miss the next red-hot reads from Temptation's BLAZE:

#679 PRIVATE PLEASURES
Janelle Denison

#682 PRIVATE FANTASIES
Janelle Denison

#686 SEDUCING SULLIVAN
Julie Elizabeth Leto

FANTASY
Lori Foster

Harlequin Books

TORONTO • NEW YORK • LONDON
AMSTERDAM • PARIS • SYDNEY • HAMBURG
STOCKHOLM • ATHENS • TOKYO • MILAN
MADRID • WARSAW • BUDAPEST • AUCKLAND

This book is dedicated to Susan Sheppard, Editor Extraordinaire. Your wit, intelligence and incredible talent make writing a truly pleasurable endeavor. You have my thanks.

ISBN 0-373-25775-9

FANTASY

Printed in U.S.A.

1

"GOING ONCE...going twice..."

With anticipation thick in the air, the announcer called out, "Sold!"

And Sebastian Sinclair watched as the man just purchased was led off the stage to the sounds of raucous feminine cheers. Soon it would be his turn.

How the hell did I get myself talked into this? he wondered. Wearing a suit, watching huge amounts of money change hands with no consideration of the cost, being the center of attention—he hated it all. It reminded him of his youth and the fact that he had nothing in common with these shallow blue bloods.

Most of all, he hated the idea of being bought like an expensive toy for the amusement of rich women—regardless of the cause.

He seemed to be the only male not thrilled with the prospect of displaying himself. The others, in ages varying from late twenties to early forties, were smiling, flaunting their wares, so to speak, and generally getting into the spirit of the thing. Only one man remained in line before Sebastian now and judging by the brawn of the guy and his rough-whiskered chin, he wouldn't last long. The women were really going berserk on the macho ones.

Which was probably why the construction workers had on very snug, tattered jeans and T-shirts too tight for men half their size—an adjustment for their female audience, no doubt. There was absolutely no way a man could work comfortably in a shirt that tight.

Likewise, the landscapers wore their work boots and jeans, some of them with no shirts on at all. And the carpenter—he had a heavy tool belt hanging low on his hips. The ensemble was complete with wrenches, a nail pouch, and the largest hammer Sebastian had ever seen, no doubt a pitiful attempt at symbolism. Sebastian shook his head and tried, without much success, to mask his amusement.

The announcer, a woman with a very wide, toothy smile, led a man around the stage by one finger hooked in his belt loop. The audience roared, then roared again when she had him turn, showing him to advantage. The spotlight moved over his backside and feminine shrieks filled the air.

Sebastian wondered if any of these rich people realized the seriousness of the benefit, the purpose the money would serve in assisting abused women. He doubted it. To them, it was a lark, not a humanitarian deed to build shelters and help those in need.

To Sebastian, it was much more personal.

The brawny guy ahead of him bounded onstage, anxious for his turn to titillate the giggling masses, and

Sebastian was left with a female attendant, waiting for his cue.

As he'd guessed, the bewhiskered fellow went quickly, the last bid coming on a crescendo of womanly squeals and bawdy jests. The attendant took Sebastian's arm and directed him forward.

As he reached the center of the stage, hot lighting flooded over him. He stared out at the audience, satisfied with their reckless spending, but thoroughly disgusted by their careless attitudes. None of them gave a thought to where the money would go or how badly it was needed. They were all the same, full of glitz and shine; shallow, frivolous, concentrating only on their own pleasures. He was disdainful of them all.

And then he saw her.

She stood alone, a small dark-haired woman with huge eyes that dominated her face and expressed her fascination. She didn't smile as he met her stare. She didn't yell out suggestions or a bid as the other women were doing. She didn't laugh or joke; she didn't do anything but watch him. He no longer heard the announcer, no longer felt the heat of the bright lights. His boredom and disinterest seemed to melt away. Her face was upturned, her lips slightly parted, as if in surprise. And he knew—she *couldn't* look away. Somehow he held her physically by the connection of their gazes.

Sebastian didn't dare blink. She seemed awestruck and innocent and he found her utterly irresistible. For some insane reason, because something inside him had stirred and heated at the sight of her, he had no intention of letting her go.

Maybe he wouldn't berate Shay after all. He just might end up thanking her.

SHE WANTED HIM.

Brandi stood in the middle of the floor, right beneath the stage. The men had been coming and going, none of them overly remarkable to her mind, but then, she wasn't here to buy a man. She was only attending this benefit to support her sister, Shay. In truth, she avoided gatherings like this one, where the testosterone filled the air so thick you could choke on it. And there were any number of ways she would have preferred to spend her birthday.

But none of that mattered at the moment. The man onstage was incredible, and once her gaze locked with his, she couldn't stop staring. She felt an irresistible connection to him, and she couldn't seem to find the wit—or the will—to walk away.

The woman handling the bids chuckled at some jest Brandi had missed, then turned to catch the man's arm. Holding a microphone in one hand, she gripped his arm firmly with the other and cuddled up to him. "Such a generous bid!" she called out sounding very excited, though Brandi, deeply involved in her own scrutiny, hadn't heard the exact amount offered. "He's worth every penny, ladies! Come on now, don't be shy. This one is quite a specimen." She squeezed his upper arm, testing his muscle, then made an "oohing" expression to the audience.

The man didn't look overly complimented. He looked disdainful, and rather than work toward drawing more attention to himself as the other men had, he merely crossed his arms and braced his long legs apart. He seemed impossibly tall and strong and masculine in his rigid stance. As impenetrable as a stone wall. Almost barbaric in his strength. And he continued to look at Brandi.

The announcer struggled to gain his cooperation. She tried to force him into a turn, wanting to display him as she had the others in order to raise the already astronomical sum they'd collected. He resisted her efforts with ease. The announcer couldn't budge him a single inch.

And the women loved it. They called out more bids, made explicit suggestions on what they'd do with him and haggled amongst themselves.

Brandi's fascination built. Never before had she felt it, at least, not in eight long years. And before that, she'd simply been too young. But there was no denying the interest surging inside her now. She'd made a decision earlier that day, a decision that would change her life—hopefully for the better. But this? Could she really consider bidding on a man? On *this* man?

In answer to her own thoughts, she shook her head no.

The man gave her a slight, devastating smile that stole her breath—and then slowly nodded his head yes, as if to encourage her. Embarrassed color flooded her face. He couldn't possibly know what she'd been thinking! She shook her head again, more emphatically this time, but that only made his smile widen until he gave her a full-fledged grin.

God, he was gorgeous.

And big. Too big. Much, much too big and imposing and... Brandi felt her heartbeat trip, felt heat wash over her, as if someone had opened an oven. She tried to step back, to break the invisible connection between them, but she couldn't manage it. Never in her life had she been the object of such masculine notice. Her sister Shay was so striking—tall and pale and beautiful beyond words—Brandi naturally faded beside her, becoming a mere shadow to Shay's impressive height and inexhaustible energy.

But now a man—this incredible mountain of a man—had latched on to her with his bold gaze and he wouldn't release her. She felt both alarmed and pleasantly flustered.

At that moment, Shay reappeared at her side. Her slim eyebrows lifted in a question. The man's gaze automatically reverted to Shay, who towered over Brandi.

It wasn't quite jealousy that Brandi felt—she and Shay were very close—it was more like resignation. She had no business staring at a man, inviting his interest when she had no intention of returning it. She *couldn't* return it, not yet, and certainly not with a man like him. Her resolution to start this birthday off differently hadn't yet been implemented. And it never would be with a man like him.

Now that he wasn't looking at her, she could look away, too, and did—with a deep, regretful sigh.

Shay heard that sigh and smiled. "He is gorgeous, isn't he?"

Burdened with her own thoughts, Brandi turned to look up at Shay and asked stupidly, "Who?"

"The man you've been ogling." Then Shay took her arm and led her away from the center of the floor. "Every woman here has been doing the same. But then, he's not exactly the type of man any red-blooded female would fail to notice."

"He isn't enjoying being on that stage."

Shay chuckled. "No, I don't think he is. But did you see how the women are reacting to his disinterest? They're going wild for him."

Feeling choked, Brandi said, "Then I suppose he'll bring in a good amount for your charity auction."

"That's what I'm counting on." Shay slanted Brandi a look. "I could make you a loan, you know."

Brandi stumbled but quickly righted herself. "Good grief, Shay! You're not suggesting...?"

"Why not?"

Such a ridiculous question hardly deserved an answer, but it irritated Brandi enough to give one anyway. "You already know why. Did you look at him? He's bigger than a barn and dark as Satan. Even wearing a suit, the man looks like a disgruntled savage. And so far, he's only smiled once."

"Yes, but that smile almost knocked you on your can. I watched the whole thing. Admit it, Brandi, you like what you saw."

Trying to be reasonable, Brandi explained, "He makes my insides jumpy. That's not a good sign."

Shay's face lit up. "Are you kidding? That's a fantastic sign!"

"No."

"But..."

"No buts." Then Brandi softened her tone. She knew Shay only had her best interests at heart, and she wanted to put her at ease. "I made a decision this morning to get my life in order, to start...circulating again."

"Circulating? As in dating?" There was both caution and elation in Shay's tone.

Brandi smiled. "Yes. I'll probably make a fool of myself, and I'll have to start out with someone safe, someone I know well and can trust and who isn't too pushy or overbearing. But it's past time I got on with my life. I'm going to start acting like a normal woman again if it kills me."

Shay grinned. "Well, I don't think death will actually be a by-product. And I'm thrilled with your decision, I really am. But since you already like the guy onstage—"

They both turned as the announcer began responding to a volley of bids. Things were winding up. He'd be sold any second now. Sadly, Brandy shook her head. Shay didn't understand. No one in her family did. She tried her best not to burden them, so she kept her lingering difficulties to herself and merely replied, "Fine," whenever they chanced to ask how she was doing. So far, that seemed to satisfy everyone.

Brandi turned away from the stage, unwilling to witness the final bid. "I'd never buy a man, Shay. I couldn't do it. You know that."

Shay stared down at her, then straightened to her full, impressive height. "Well, I certainly have no problem with it."

And before Brandi could stop her, before she could get a single word out of her suddenly dry mouth, Shay raised her arm and in a loud, carrying voice called out a bid well above any other they'd heard that night.

Stunned silence followed that astronomical bid, quickly replaced by loud complaints and feminine groans. But no one could go any higher. And after a moment, the announcer banged her gavel with obvious satisfaction. "Sold! To Shay Sommers, and pound for pound, he's a hell of a bargain!"

THE VAGARIES OF FATE were often rather hideous.

Brandi closed her eyes a moment, denying her own despair.

"Well," Shay said, her tone incredibly dry, "that was taken care of rather easily, wasn't it? No one even bothered to counter with a higher bid."

Brandi opened her eyes with that bit of nonsense. "Are you crazy, Shay? Have you totally lost your mind? You can have any man you want, *any* man! You certainly don't need to pay for them."

"But I wanted that man." Then Shay waved an elegant hand, avoiding Brandi's gaze. "This is my event. My project. Everyone expected me to make a purchase."

Brandi made a choking sound.

"Oh come on, Brandi. It's the same as donating the money directly. Only this way, the men on stage get to advertise their businesses to all the press that's here, displaying themselves as concerned businessmen, and the shelter will benefit since every company represented has promised to donate free labor. They'll do painting, concrete work, landscaping...whatever, to help get the newest shelter up and running. They get great publicity and we get free labor. Everyone is happy."

Except me, Brandi thought, feeling categorically unhappy. She wondered what Shay's man would contribute, but in the next instant, decided she didn't want to know. One could only guess what a big, unsmiling barbarian like him did for a living.

"It's a business venture," Shay continued. "Everyone will come out ahead—even the travel agency that donated the Gatlinburg prize packages because it's fabulous publicity for them. And a lot of the people using the packages will be repeat customers. But most of all, needy families will get housing. Do you realize how much money we've made?"

Brandi understood Shay's enthusiasm. Ever since

she'd been widowed, Shay had done her best to become involved in the elite Jackson community of Tennessee, trying to pull resources from the wealthy to help those in need. She had her husband's money, which gave her a lot of clout, and she had the energy and wit to put it to good use. Unfortunately, Shay didn't fit the part of the matronly widow, not with her exceptional looks and outgoing personality. Many of the men refused to take her efforts seriously, and many of the women chose to see her as a personal threat.

Brandi knew her sister wanted desperately to find a purpose in life, some way to make use of the fortune her husband had left behind. And Brandi wanted to support her in every way she could.

"Shay," Brandi said, not wanting to dim her sister's overwhelming exuberance, "You don't owe me any explanations. If you want to buy a man...well, you can certainly afford it and I had no business questioning you. I apologize." She *was* sorry—sorry she'd ever come here tonight. Now all she wanted to do was go home, eat her birthday cake in private and forget she'd ever seen him.

Shay grinned. "I just wanted to make certain you understood my motives."

Brandi nodded. She did understand. They'd made a bundle tonight, but then she'd never doubted they would. Whenever her sister set out to do something it got done, in a big way.

This time Shay had bought herself a very expensive man.

Without really meaning to, Brandi asked, "But why him?" There were any number of men Shay could have chosen and each and every one of them would have been thrilled with her as purchaser. So why had she chosen this particular man? The one man Brandi wished she'd had the nerve to buy for herself.

Not that it mattered. Brandi instinctively avoided men like him. He was too large, too dark and too imposing. Even under his suit, she'd been able to see all that hard muscle. The man was a damn behemoth, a huge warrior looking ready for battle. Brandi had no idea what she'd do with him if she had him.

But several ideas, vague in nature, flitted through her mind.

Shay only smiled. "You saw for yourself how incredibly sexy he is."

Sexy didn't even come close to describing him. He'd looked at her, and she'd gone warm and nervous and breathless all at the same time. He hadn't flexed or winked or done any of the things the other men had done. He'd merely stood there, looking magnificent.

And Shay had bought him.

Catching Brandi's hand and dragging her along, Shay led her to where the men were being introduced to the women who'd had the final bids. Brandi tried to hold back, but Shay wouldn't allow it.

"Come on, Brandi. Our guy should be somewhere at the end of the line. He was the last one sold."

Our guy? The heels of her low black pumps left marks on the tile floor as Brandi dug in, refusing to move another inch. "Now wait just a minute, Shay! I don't know what you're up to, but he's not *our* guy."

With a tug, Shay got her moving again. "You're right. He's yours."

2

"YOU CAN STOP right now, Shay. I want no part of this."

"Now Brandi," Shay whispered, leaning way down to reach Brandi's ear. "The press is everywhere, just as I'd hoped. You don't want to give my charity event a bad name, do you? You know how much trouble I already have getting these stuffy old snobs to accept me and to take part in the benefits. If Phillip hadn't left me a very wealthy widow, none of them would even speak to me. And if it wasn't for something so outlandish as an auction, not one of them would have parted with a single additional dime. They couldn't care less about the needy, you know that, but they do love to have their fun. I had to find a way to give them that in the name of charity—to entice them. You know how crowded the women's shelters are here in Jackson. We need this auction to succeed. But if my own sister acts appalled, I'll never be elected to spearhead another event."

Brandi ground her teeth in frustration, but had to admit Shay was right. It was important to show her support, which was why she'd attended the auction in the first place. Ever since Phillip's death, Shay had thrown herself into other activities, but this was the first time she'd made much headway. And the auction was an undeniable success. It would be the event that would open future opportunities for Shay. She wanted to help; she needed to help.

The very idea of women purchasing men had all kinds of connotations attached, just as Shay had predicted. Which was why an abundance of reporters had also attended, titillated and ready to produce a story that would give the auction the publicity it needed.

Brandi couldn't begin to imagine what Shay had in mind for her man. She wasn't sure she wanted to know. For some reason, the idea of Shay alone with him on a quiet, romantic getaway disturbed her. And as much as she hated to admit it, as much as she loved her sister and wanted her to be happy, she felt envious.

"Come on, Brandi. You'll enjoy this."

Extremely doubtful, she thought but it was difficult to take your sister to task when she was so incredibly tall. Compared to Brandi's five feet four inches, Shay's six feet could be rather persuasive.

They finally stopped beside a large crowd of women waiting to claim their "purchases." Brandi looked around, seeing men and women pairing off while photographers captured every move. The women postured, showing off their elegant gowns and jewels, and the men smiled, looking sexy and confident and proud of their success. They were all so natural, so outgoing...so different from her.

Her gaze skimmed the room, taking it all in. Everyone seemed to be having a good time.

All but one man.

Brandi froze, her gaze glued to that intense, unsmiling face. Size alone distinguished him from the other men. But there was also the darkness about him, his straight black hair, his tanned skin. Only his green eyes seemed bright, and they were like fire—watching her.

Already he'd loosened his tie and unbuttoned the top of his white dress shirt. Dark curling hair showed in the opening. Brandi wondered if he was that hairy all over, then flushed with the thought.

Lounging, with one broad shoulder propped against the wall, he affected a casual pose, but Brandi suspected there was nothing casual about it. A panther tensed to attack his prey was a better comparison than casual negligence.

He might as well have been on the stage again, he so completely dominated her vision, her thoughts. A touch of thrilling excitement swirled in her belly.

And then it hit her.

He was now Shay's companion for the next five days, but was singling Brandi out by staring, stalking her with his eyes. Brandi stiffened and let her own black brows draw down in a frown. The man must be a complete cad! Of course, she was searching for reasons to dislike him, to make the situation more tolerable, but still, she had a valid point.

The corner of his mouth quirked in amusement for a split second, then leveled out again. His green gaze, brighter now, but still so very warm, slid over her face, then over the rest of her.

She remembered that look, knew what it meant, though it had been years since she'd experienced it. Experiencing it now made her stomach flip and her muscles tighten. She wondered if her plain black shift disappointed him. It fell to just below her knees, then met with her black stockings. With a barely scooped neck and elbow length sleeves, the dress exemplified her life—plain, uncomplicated, quiet.

Just as she had wanted it to be.

Several women were attempting to speak to him, but he ignored them. He pushed himself away from the wall and started toward Brandi. She considered making a hasty exit, leaving Shay to fend for herself. Watching the two of them get acquainted wasn't something she could anticipate with any degree of outward indifference.

But Shay turned then and followed Brandi's gaze. She placed a restraining hand on Brandi's shoulder, and as the man reached them Shay embraced him with her free arm, kissing his cheek with familiar affection. Brandi could only gawk.

"Sebastian, you did wonderfully—our biggest attraction! For a moment there, I was afraid my bid would cause a brawl. Some of the ladies were very disappointed to be put out of the running." She laughed, then added, "I was right—you are a natural."

"A natural idiot for letting you talk me into this," he said easily, his gaze swinging down to Brandi. He studied her, and his tone dropped to an intimate level.

"I don't think I'll thank you for making that last bid, Shay."

Brandi's eyes widened. Was he insinuating that he'd wanted *her* to bid? She opened her mouth to...say what? She had no idea, but then he glanced at Shay again.

"I'd appreciate an introduction," he said, "since you two seem well acquainted."

Shay grinned, making no effort to hide her satisfaction at his interest. "Not only well acquainted, but related. Sebastian, I'd like you to meet my little sister." She pressed Brandi forward. "Sebastian Sinclair, meet Brandi Sommers."

"Sister?" He looked surprised and his eyes narrowed on Brandi's face, scrutinizing her every feature. Brandi knew he was drawing comparisons between her and Shay, and she was bound to come up lacking. She stiffened her spine and scowled at him.

Shay forged on, intent on some course that eluded Brandi. But somehow Brandi knew, she wasn't going to like it.

"Sebastian is a good friend of mine," Shay said, then added with a burst of wary enthusiasm, "Happy birthday, honey! I bought him for you."

SEBASTIAN'S FIRST THOUGHT was that the woman would faint dead at his feet. She'd gone deathly pale and her mouth had dropped open. Yet when he reached for her, she jerked back and there wasn't a single ounce of uncertainty in her expression.

Her glare said plain enough that she wanted nothing to do with him.

His sense of indignation rose, but he was unsure what to say. He couldn't pull his gaze away from her face, regardless of her obvious rejection. Up close, he could see her huge eyes were a very soft blue, ringed with thick black lashes. Her nose tipped up on the end and her small stubborn chin was slightly pointed. There were hollows beneath her cheekbones giving her a very delicate appearance, but her jaw was firm. Her lips...she had a very sexy mouth, he decided, lush and well defined, even if she refused to smile, even if her expression now was more shocked than pleased. She wasn't pale like Shay, but rather her skin had a dusky rose hue, and her midnight black hair...it was wildly curly, cut short and framing her face...untamable. He found himself suffering a severe case of instantaneous lust. And yet the woman looked appalled at her sister's generosity. Well, hell.

"I'd never have guessed you were related," he said, trying for an ounce of aplomb in the awkward moment. "You two look nothing alike."

Shay grinned. "I'm adopted, didn't you know? I guess I never told you about that."

"I guess you didn't."

She surprised him with that, enough that he could actually take his eyes off Brandi's face a moment to stare at Shay. "You're not kidding?"

"Nope. My stepparents thought they couldn't have

kids, so they took me in. And they've always treated me like their first child."

"You are their first child," Brandi muttered, frowning up at her sister.

"But shortly after my adoption was final, Mom got pregnant." Shay beamed down at Brandi. "She's like a miracle child."

"Hardly a child now," he said, his attention resting on Brandi's pursed lips for a few seconds. He envisioned kissing that mulish expression off her mouth, then had to force that image away before he embarrassed himself.

Brandi rolled her eyes, then crossed her arms over her breasts—small perfect breasts, he couldn't help noticing. She barely reached his collarbone, but she managed to look imposing nonetheless. "You'll have to forgive my sister, Mr. Sinclair. She gets carried away with her generous intentions on occasion. But I don't want...that is..." She fumbled for the appropriate words, which gave Shay a chance to offer more arguments.

"I can afford him, Brandi. And he's the perfect gift!" Brandi stared at her sister, and Shay grumbled defensively, "Well, he is!"

With her face bright red and her posture rigid, Brandi appeared more than determined to send him on his way.

Sebastian interrupted before she could do just that. "When you say 'little' sister, you aren't exaggerating."

Shay grasped the change of topic gratefully. "Brandi

looks like the family. Petite and dark. I'm afraid with my gawky height and fair hair, it's me who's the oddity."

"Ha!" Brandy now had her hands on her narrow hips. "A beautiful oddity and you know it." To Sebastian, she said, "Shay is the reining matriarch of the family. She does her best to boss us all around, and usually we let her because she enjoys it so much. It gives her something to do and keeps her out of trouble. But this time…"

He didn't want to be dismissed, so he held out his hand to Brandi and quickly interrupted. "So I'm a birthday present, am I? I suppose I've been worse things in my line of work."

She put her small hand in his large one, gave it two jerky, firm pumps, then mumbled, "Nice to meet you." And in the next breath she asked with a good dose of suspicion, "What exactly is your line of work?"

Shay poked Brandi in the ribs, causing her to jump. As Brandi rubbed her side, scowling, Shay explained. "Sebastian owns a personal security agency and he does a credible job of taking care of people, watching out for them, protecting them from danger of any kind. It's one reason for all the brawn you noticed."

Brandi's eyes flared and her cheeks flushed. So she'd noticed him to that degree had she? *Excellent*.

She stuttered a moment, then ended with, "I'm going to kill you, Shay."

Shay looked totally unconcerned with the threat. She fluttered her manicured hand in Brandi's direction as if to fan away the anger. "Sebastian has to stay in top shape. His job can be, at times, very physical. But he's up to it. He's real hero material, he just doesn't realize it."

"I do my job the same as anyone else, Shay. There's nothing heroic about it."

"You see what I mean?" Shay asked Brandi, then added in a stage whisper, "Actually he'd be a perfect male if he wasn't such a chauvinist. But Sebastian thinks of all women as delicate and frail and he wants to save them all."

He narrowed his eyes. "Oh, I don't know about that, Shay. I certainly wouldn't term you as delicate. Tough as shoe leather maybe, but not—"

Shay smacked at him, laughing. But Brandi frowned as if she didn't quite trust him, regardless of her sister's romanticized declaration. Then she turned to Shay, and though she lowered her voice, he heard every word. "I don't know what you're up to here, Shay, but it won't work, so stop it right now. You bought him, you can just keep him."

"I don't want him!" Shay said, frowning now herself. "He's a great guy, but we're too much alike. We'd kill each other within twenty-four hours. Besides, I've already been this route and don't intend to go it again."

"But I should?"

Shay shrugged. "You know how it is about a path never traveled. Your weeds are growing tall, Brandi.

Pretty soon you won't be able to find the path anymore."

"Oh for heaven's sake," Brandi muttered. "That's the dumbest bit of argument you've ever come up with."

Sebastian was beginning to feel like a stray mutt. Not since he was twelve years old and had begun gaining his height and physical structure had a woman showed such disinterest in his company. He wasn't vain, but then, he wasn't stupid, either. He'd had women argue over him before, plenty of times actually—but never to see who had to be stuck with him. More often than not, women chased him.

But now Brandi wasn't chasing him—she was trying to chase him away. Perversely, he was determined to hang around.

Shay had her hands on her hips, mimicking Brandi's stance, and she looked every bit as determined as Brandi. "I wanted to give you something special for your birthday, Brandi, but I was at a loss. I couldn't think of a single suitable gift. Then, well, you mentioned your new plans, and inspiration struck."

Sebastian bit his upper lip. He didn't understand the part about "new plans," but inspiration was apparently the way Brandi had stared at him while he was onstage. Her sister had interpreted that eat-him-alive look as interest, so maybe he hadn't misread her after all. Maybe it was that her interest hadn't quite encompassed five days alone with him, as the prize package specified. He didn't understand why—but he was already determined to find out.

Brandi waved a small dismissive hand—the same as her sister had done earlier, only this time it was aimed in his direction. "*He* wasn't part of my plans."

"*He's* perfect for your plans! You're twenty-six today and you never have any fun. Sebastian is fun." She glanced at him and demanded verification. "Aren't you fun, Sebastian?"

"A laugh a minute." But he didn't feel like laughing. He felt like telling Shay to be quiet and stop pushing her sister. Hell, Shay was practically forcing him on Brandi, and she was resisting admirably. It was a new experience—and he didn't like it one bit.

Brandi closed her eyes, then opened them again. "No."

"Now, Brandi..."

It was most likely male pride that motivated him, because he didn't like being rejected any more than the next guy. Especially not after Brandi had managed to intrigue him so thoroughly with her blatant, wide-eyed, somehow innocent staring. He should just forget about the whole thing. He didn't have time to take away from his other commitments. He was in the middle of screening new help for hire at his office, and each room in his home was in some stage of renovation. His free time these days amounted to nil.

But he found himself stepping in front of Brandi and Shay, hiding them from the crowd. That damn no had sounded entirely too final, and he'd already determined not to let her say no.

"I'm sorry you're not happy with the arrangement, Miss Sommers," he said, not quite able to keep the annoyance out of his tone, "but the fact is, neither of us has any choice at this point. The press is ready to snap a shot of anything that even remotely looks suspicious. If you hesitate or look as if you're being coerced, Shay's publicity will suffer. My business will suffer. The women's shelter will suffer."

Turning very slowly, Brandi stared up at him. "You're exaggerating."

"We're next in line for photos. If you look unwilling or unhappy you can imagine how the text will read below the picture. They'll slaughter your sister's intentions, and my business will be given a bum rap. They'll somehow twist it so that you had reason to refuse my company on the trip. This whole event will end up looking like a disreputable scam, and the efforts to provide housing for battered families will lose ground."

After spewing that nonsensical garbage—all of it exaggerated, just as she'd claimed—Sebastian waited. If Brandi Sommers was anything at all like her sister, she wouldn't want to jeopardize the success of the auction. He waited, holding his breath and feeling ridiculous for letting her decision matter so much to him.

After a calming breath, she looked at Shay. "What will happen now?"

A look of relief crossed Shay's features, then she smiled. "Your prize package includes a short trip to

Gatlinburg, with all expenses paid." When Brandi started to protest again, Shay added, "You'll be going to a very quiet resort. I picked the place myself. You'll love it."

Reaching out, Sebastian clasped Shay's shoulder, giving her a silent signal to desist. If he was to be forced on Brandi, he preferred to do the forcing himself. Somehow it seemed less demeaning. "Look at it this way, Miss Sommers. Like it or not, you own me for the next five days."

Her eyes grew so large he had to struggle to hide his grin. That little reminder had certainly gained her attention. "You'll be the one calling the shots. If you want to sit in the cabin the whole time and brood about your pushy sister here, that's your business. I'm just there as an escort if you want or need one." Then he added innocently, "Or for whatever purpose you assign me."

That notion had promise, even though Brandi was proving to be a contrary little wretch. She might be cute, and her unwavering gaze could set a man on fire, but she wasn't the most warm or welcoming woman he'd ever met.

Strange, but for some reason that fact wasn't deterring his interest in the least.

Brandi did look slightly intrigued by the idea, but then she shook her head. "I don't know...."

"Take your time and think about it." He added with a nod at the reporters, "But until we're out of here, it's important that you play along. At least pretend to be an excited, willing participant."

Brandi hesitated again, but she did give in. "Fine. I'll…think about it. But let's get this part of it over with, please. I'd like to get home."

Shay gave her an apologetic smile. "You can't leave any time soon. The photographers want pictures of the two of you together. There's hors d'oeuvres, drinks. Dancing."

Brandi stiffened up again. For whatever reason, she was determined to resist the attraction between them.

He was just as determined not to let her.

BRANDI CONTEMPLATED muzzling her sister. She was in fine form tonight, at her most autocratic. "We'll do a few pictures, Shay. But you can forget the dancing and drinks."

Shay looked annoyed, but Sebastian accepted her edict. "Fair enough. Are you ready?" He held out his hand to Brandi.

Ready? Good God, no, she wasn't ready. But at this point, Shay had left her little choice.

She really didn't want to touch him again. That one brief handshake had been enough to give her goose-flesh. Just looking at him made her heart beat faster. But she took his hand anyway. It was so large, it swallowed her smaller one. She noticed again that his palm was callused, his skin warm and dry. She actually liked touching him this way. Somehow, the gesture felt right. But she knew getting close enough to that big body to dance—to let him hold her—would be a mistake. She'd probably make a fool of herself and she couldn't bear that. Not with him.

Better to discourage him now; it would save them both a lot of aggravation.

Shay had disappeared after the first picture—she was probably hiding. She'd dumped a volatile situation in Brandi's lap with no warning, and though Brandi knew Shay meant well, Brandi was now in the unenviable position of turning down a sinfully gorgeous, sexy man.

"Mr. Sinclair..."

"Sebastian."

She faltered just a moment, then nodded. "Uh, right. Sebastian." She looked around the room, avoiding his direct gaze. "I can understand the need to protect Shay's reputation by going through with a few harmless photos. But there's no point in carrying this farce any further than that. The idea of a trip together is absurd."

"No, it isn't."

She frowned at his firm disagreement, but he didn't give her a chance to argue. He towered over her, his expression mild, his tone calm.

"Your sister has made me your gift. By now, everyone here knows it. If we tried to avoid the trip, someone would surely find out and the auction would lose its credibility." He tilted his head at her. "Why are you so set against going?"

Since she couldn't very well tell him the truth, she

mustered up her most sarcastic tone. "Gee, let's see. I've just met a total stranger and now I'm supposed to go off on a private trip with him."

He only grinned at her, amused by her forced acerbity. Brandi sighed. Well, so much for insulting him. "Mr....Sebastian. I don't know you. I don't know anything about you."

"Funny, but with the way you stared earlier, I assumed you'd be pleased to have my company."

She drew herself up, which was pathetic given the fact she stood at least a foot shorter than him. "You put yourself on a stage for just that purpose! Besides, I wasn't the only one watching you."

"But you are about the only one who'd cause such a fuss over a free vacation package! I think just about any other woman here tonight would be happy to go."

"Maybe I should just give one of them my *gift* then, and you can both be deliriously happy."

He stood glaring down at her for a moment, then his expression cleared and he chuckled. He had a nice chuckle...for a mountain. "Damn, I can't believe I'm standing here debating this with you. Talk about a blow to the old masculine ego." He took her arm and, without asking, led her toward a quieter corner. "I suppose if I must be abused, I ought to at least find some privacy so I can salvage a little pride."

Now Brandi felt totally flustered. Abused? She certainly hadn't meant to abuse him. But she also didn't want privacy. She wanted to go home to her quiet apartment and pretend none of this had happened. But

looking around, she realized they were drawing notice, so she allowed him to drag her away.

When they stopped in the corner Sebastian mo-
tioned for her to seat herself at a wooden bench there.
She did, and then he sprawled beside her, taking up
too much room, letting his thigh touch hers. Brandi
stiffened. "Mr....Sebastian. I'm sorry if I've insulted
you in any way. Really. That was never my intent. It's
just that I don't like being forced into a corner."

He stared at her for a moment before he seemed to
come to some sort of decision. "I have to tell you,
Brandi. Your attitude really surprises me."

"Oh?" She didn't want him delving too deeply into
her *attitude*, so she said, "You're used to strange
women jumping at the chance to go off alone with
you?"

"I wouldn't exactly call you strange. A little different, maybe. But then again... No, don't storm off in a
huff." He caught her arm and eased her back into her
seat. "I was only teasing."

His smile was so catching, she almost smiled, too.

"You know I'm your sister's friend. I assume you
trust her?"

"Of course I do. She's my sister."

"Then you know I can't be a totally reprehensible
character or Shay, who has no tolerance for unkindness
in any form, wouldn't have bought me for you. Correct?"

Exasperation overrode her annoyance. "Good grief.
You aren't exactly a packaged present, for heaven's

sake. It's a donation is all. You make yourself sound like a toy to play with."

He chuckled and Brandi felt her face turn hot as she realized what she'd said. He reached out and touched her cheek with his knuckles, softly, just brushing her skin. Brandi almost shot off her seat.

"I don't know how much playing I'm up to, Brandi, but I'll try not to aggravate you too much."

His mere presence aggravated her, but not the way he assumed. She cleared her throat. "I didn't mean to insinuate..."

"I know." He took his taunting knuckles away. "Now, back to dissecting my character. Shay told you I own a personal protection agency. People, the majority being politicians or those with high-profile positions, hire me as a bodyguard, or to keep watch over various functions where they might expect trouble. But I also take on other, more personal cases, with endangered women or children. It never ceases to amaze me how men can so easily brutalize someone smaller than themselves."

Brandi shivered. There was a savagery in his eyes as he spoke that unnerved her. She had no doubt of the contempt he felt for bullies; but then, she shared that contempt.

He seemed drawn into his own thoughts for a moment, then he continued. "I was trained by the military. Spent eight years with Uncle Sam on special assignments that included keeping guard over some big government officials. Then I bailed out, worked for a firm for two years, and now I own my own business. I don't like people who hurt or frighten other people. So I've made it my job to stop people who do."

"How?"

"Excuse me?"

She had to ask. She had to know. "How do you stop them?"

His teeth closed over his upper lip and he pinned her with his gaze, refusing to let her look away. "However I have to. Without violence whenever possible. With extreme violence when necessary."

She shuddered, but otherwise hid her reaction. For some reason, having him give her the unvarnished truth lessened the impact of his ruthless words. Brandi glanced at him, then muttered, "At least you're honest."

"Always."

The drop in his voice nearly did her in. It was almost as if he suffered the same confusing mix of emotions that she did. Of course that was impossible. Her situation was unique to women; a man wouldn't understand.

"I'll always be honest with you, Brandi. As you get to know me—"

"I don't want to get to know you."

"—you'll learn that I never lie."

She wanted to growl in frustration. No man had ever so diligently pursued her. She'd given him options, offered to let him out of the absurd situation. Yet he remained insistent. "What do you get out of this, Sebastian?"

"Other than your sterling company?"

There was that touch of mockery again. She lifted her chin. "Yes. Why would you allow yourself to be sold in the first place? You seemed...disgusted by it all."

"I was, a little." Then he smiled. "Actually, a lot. I'm not one for rich crowds. Especially since my job usually keeps me in the shadows. And throwing money away—"

"On a very good cause."

"I agree. But the battered women's shelter wasn't the motivation for most of the bids. Even without the cause, those people would have been comfortable tossing away thousands of dollars. To them it was no more than a lark, and the waste of it sickens me."

"So, why would you do it if you hated it so much?"

"Because the money is desperately needed. Because the number of battered women and abused children rises every day. I see it in my job, I live with it. And I knew, with Shay in charge, the auction would be a success. She refused my check because she needed bodies to fill the stage. And when Shay sets her mind on something, she can be pretty damn persuasive."

Brandi drew a sigh, then shook her head. He was a likable man, whether she wanted to like him or not. He was mostly polite, even with his arrogance, and his motivations certainly weren't suspect. If anything, she had to admire his sense of obligation. "Shay has always been a bully. I swear, when she wants something, there's no stopping her."

"She's pushy, but she's also a shrewd business-woman."

"You know my sister well?"

"I thought I did. But that bit about adoption threw me. She never let on."

"Shay doesn't think about it all that much, none of us do. She's my older sister. My parents' first child. Besides, it's not something you'd bring up in idle conversation."

"I suppose."

"How did the two of you meet?" Even as she asked it, Brandi knew she was putting her nose where it had no business being. The notion that Shay and Sebastian might have once had a relationship was irrelevant to her. Or at least it should be.

But she didn't retract the question.

"Shay and I've been friends a little over a year now. I had a case where a man threatened his wife. He'd beaten her before, and the hospital had records of the times she'd been in. But she had two kids, no money and no place else to go. Shay had just started work at the shelter. I got the mother and children settled there, then I worked with a few friends on the police force to get the guy locked up. I would have preferred a more personal vengeance, but that wouldn't have solved the problem long-term. As it turned out, we discovered he was dealing drugs, too, so he's out of the picture for a good long while. Anyway, Shay was great, making the family comfortable. We've had joint interests ever since."

Brandi's heart thudded against her ribs. He'd just given her incredible insight into his character, showing her his morals and his priorities. It was amazing, but she suddenly trusted him. This man was a protector, a man of honor.

And he'd offered to let her be the boss. It was such an intriguing notion—one that worked nicely with her plan to take charge of her life and move forward. She knew now, without a single doubt, he'd abide by her rules.

She hadn't figured out exactly what her rules would be yet, but she had time to worry about that. With a burst of unusual confidence, she decided to take the chance. She thrust her hand toward him and waited.

He looked at her, then at her hand. One glossy black eyebrow lifted, and there was amusement in his green eyes. He took her hand. "What are we shaking on?"

"I'll go to the resort with you."

"Ah." His grin was wide, putting deep dimples into his lean cheeks. "It was the lulling sound of my voice that brought you around, wasn't it? The practiced way I repeat a story? No? Then you were convinced by the way I sprawl so elegantly in a seat?"

She gave him her own grin, feeling somewhat smug. "Actually, Mr. Sinclair, I understand now that you can be trusted to stick to your word. You said I'd be the boss, and that for all intents and purposes, I own you for the next five days. I realized I couldn't possibly pass up such an opportunity. But I won't let you forget, *I'm* the one in charge."

His dark lashes lowered until she couldn't see his eyes, but his grin was still in place. "Believe me, honey. I won't be able to forget."

3

THINGS WERE MOVING too quickly. The plane wasn't at all crowded, especially in first class where Shay had put them, but the emptiness only added to Brandi's growing anxiety. Looking out the window, Brandi could see a light rain falling. She hated flying at night. She hated flying, period, but at least this was a rational fear shared by millions.

Which offered her not one bit of comfort.

Flexing her shoulders, she tried to relieve some of the tension, but that only caused her to bump into Sebastian. The man took up too much space with his large frame and even larger masculinity. When he was there, he was...*there*, and it simply wasn't possible to ignore his presence.

Shay hadn't given them much time to prepare for the trip, presumably because she thought Brandi might chicken out. Not that she would have. She was determined to see things through. But Shay wasn't taking any chances. She'd seen to every single detail—and she'd gone overboard in the luxury department.

She'd sent a retainer back to Brandi's house to pack her bags and bring them to the hotel where the auction had been held. The flight had been scheduled only a few hours after Brandi agreed to go. A limo had taken them to the airport, and a limo would await them when they landed, to whisk them off to the resort. There would be a rental car at their disposal.

Sebastian had planned on leaving the auction with a woman, so he'd brought his luggage with him. Before they'd left, he'd changed into a pair of khaki slacks and a black polo shirt. Brandi had been too flustered at the rush to pay much attention to his new attire at first. But now, with nothing to distract her from the impending flight, she looked him over.

His biceps were massive, stretching the short sleeves of the shirt. The dark color caused his green eyes to look even greener and the fit emphasized his broad muscled chest. The pants, stretched taut by his sprawl, emphasized...

Brandi jerked her gaze upward. A black-banded watch circled his thick wrist, and the shadow of his beard was now more pronounced. She jumped when he said her name.

"What?"

He opened his hand palm up on the elbow rest. "Nervous?"

She didn't accept his gesture. She couldn't. To do so would have been admitting to a weakness. And she'd gotten too good at denying her fears to admit to one of them now—not even a small one. "About what?"

"I don't know." His voice was quiet, calming, his expression very intent. She had the feeling he knew exactly how to soothe a person; his movements were too practiced and perfect. "Everything—me, the trip, the flight."

Twisting in her seat she looked at him more fully. Many of the other passengers were napping and had turned out their lights. His face was shadowed, exaggerating the sharp cut of his jaw, the high bridge of his straight nose. The deep awareness in his green eyes.

There was absolutely no chance of Brandi falling asleep.

She frowned in suspicion. "Shay told you how I feel about flying, didn't she?"

"Yeah." He stared down at her. "It's no big deal. I have my own store of phobias. Maybe some day I'll tell you about them."

This hulking mass of muscle was admitting to fears? The mountain had phobias? Brandi couldn't quite believe it. "You're kidding, right?"

"Nope." He wiggled his fingers. "Now give me your hand. It helps, I swear."

The plane began taxiing toward the runway and Brandi hastily slipped her hand into his. His skin felt incredibly hot against her chilled fingers. She looked down in surprise.

Sebastian smiled. "Your fingers are like ice."

"It's cold in here." Dumb, to sound so defensive about such a ridiculous thing. But his heat was seeping into her, making her tingle, making her breathless. She tried to moderate herself and take a more reasonable tone. "I can't believe you're so...hot."

Oh, great going, Brandi. Now she'd amused him. She

could tell by his slight smile and the teasing glint in his eyes. Still, he didn't provoke her. When he spoke, his words were soft and even. "Most men naturally have a higher body temperature than women. Probably has something to do with muscle density." He flexed his hand, turning it over so that his was on top. "I've always loved a woman's hands. They're small and delicate, but usually pretty damn strong." He squeezed her hand gently. "Yours is nice."

Brandi stared at him. That low rough voice of his could be lethal, and she suspected he knew it. He examined her hand as if he'd never seen one before. All that attention was making her stomach jumpy again, although now, the feeling was somewhat pleasant. "What are you up to?"

He chuckled. "You think I'm trying to seduce you?"

She blanched. He could fluster her with a look, but the things he said... Feeling like a fool, she shrugged. "I don't know. I'm not...used to this sort of thing."

He smiled. "Actually, I was only trying to distract you while the damn plane got off the ground. And it worked, didn't it?"

Stunned, she turned to look out the window, and found only endless black sky. She drew a deep breath and faced him again. "Yes. Thank you."

"Good." He turned to look at her more fully, unhooking his seat belt with one hand and glancing around to make certain no one could hear them. Since most everyone was sleeping, they had some measure of privacy. Brandi released him to undo her own belt, all the while watching the way he moved, the way his shoulders flexed, how his straight dark hair brushed his collar and fell over his brow. She'd never been so intrigued by a man, by his smallest movement or gesture.

She wanted to hold his hand again. In fact, there were other places she wanted to touch him besides his hands. But it could be so risky....

"Now, about seducing you..."

Good lord, it wasn't a topic to discuss. "Sebastian, really, there's absolutely no need..."

"Yes, there is. I want you to understand that I won't pressure you in any way. I know this vacation is set up to be romantic, but it doesn't have to be if that's not what you want. We can do whatever you like. Take walks, play chess, hell, you can tell me to leave you completely alone if that's what you want. But if you decide you want anything from me—"

"I won't!" The protest sounded panicked even to her own ears.

"You'll have to tell me. What we're doing now, talking and getting to know each other, that isn't about sex, okay? It's about getting comfortable with each other. I know you didn't want to come on this trip, but I'm glad you did. So if I do anything or say anything that in any way makes you uneasy, I want you to tell me. Agreed?"

Again, she chewed her lip, then nodded. He was touching on a topic she hadn't expected to have to face. Especially not this soon. Now that he'd brought it up, though, she couldn't help thinking, wondering what *he'd* think if he knew precisely why she'd been so resistant to the vacation.

He wanted her to tell him if she wanted anything? She'd never have the nerve. But now she really wished she did.

SEBASTIAN'S ARM WAS NUMB, but he didn't mind. He liked having her sleep against his side. The limo rode smoothly, the air was quiet and he liked seeing her this way—relaxed, without those impenetrable mental shields to protect her.

He looked down at her, carefully tucked a wayward curl behind her ear, then touched her smooth warm cheek. Being asleep, she didn't jump away or show her displeasure over his touch.

Having her this close was playing havoc with his libido. She had one leg tucked beneath her, so her dress had hiked up, her knees were peeking out at him and he could see a bit of pale thigh. The sight held his attention for a long moment. One of her shoes had fallen off and he pondered how tiny that foot looked next to his own size fourteens. Her foot was slim, high arched... Good grief, he could hardly believe such a thing could arouse him, but there was no denying the stirring of desire.

He was in bad shape when a woman's foot turned him on.

Warm breath bathed his throat as she sighed deeply in her sleep. Her nose touched just below his jaw, her unruly hair tickled his cheek and one small plump breast pressed into his ribs.

The stirring grew until he had a devil of a time ignoring the reactions of his own body. But she was tuckered out, poor little thing, probably as much emotionally as physically, and he had no intention of waking her. The plane ride had been difficult enough; she didn't need to know how much he wanted her. Especially since the feeling didn't appear to be mutual.

They'd only been in the limo for a little over fifteen minutes when she'd passed out. She didn't fade out gradually like most people did. No, when Brandi went to sleep it was like watching someone faint dead away. One minute she'd been sitting stiff at his side and staring out the window at the moon-shadowed scenery, the next she had slumped into him, giving him all of her slight weight.

He wanted to pull her into his lap, to cuddle her...to kiss her. She was by far the most intrinsically sensual woman he'd ever known. And when she suddenly wakened, stretching along his side like a cat and yawning hugely, he couldn't stop himself from giving her a light hug.

Her eyes snapped open and she jerked away from him. Well, he'd expected as much. She was sexy, but she wasn't interested in him.

Sebastian forced a smile. "I hope the nap helped."

"How long have I been sleeping?"

Her eyes were huge, wary, almost accusing. "About forty minutes. We should be at the lodge soon."

She fussed beside him, smoothing down her hair, tugging at the hem of her dress, rubbing her hands together. Watching her made him want her, so he looked away.

"Are you okay?"

The hesitant question had him turning toward her again. "I'm fine. Why?"

"I don't know. You seem...tense."

Tense and aroused and...almost needy. She'd tied him into more knots tonight than he'd ever experienced while growing up dirt-poor. He'd suffered plenty of rejections as a child and he'd grown accustomed to them. But as an adult, he hadn't allowed anyone to make him feel this way. He *gave* assistance, he didn't *need* it.

But now he wanted a woman who didn't want him back. The idea didn't sit well with his adult pride. So he gave her only a partial truth.

"I'm not comfortable with all this luxury. The first-class tickets, the limo. The money could have been better spent elsewhere."

For once her expression softened and the look she gave him had him struggling for breath. He had to swallow back a groan. The driver of the limo was silent behind his privacy window, set on his course. The shadowy darkness of the car and the quiet of the night only added to the intimacy of the whole enterprise. And if she didn't quit looking at him like that, he'd lose control.

Brandi didn't appear to notice his trouble. "I'm sure

our vacation plan is more extravagant than anyone else's. But then that's Shay—extravagant to a fault, especially with the people she loves. I knew the minute she decided to involve me in the trip, she'd take a personal interest. I wouldn't be surprised if everything was top of the line." Then she tilted her head. "Does it really bother you so much? Most people would love to be pampered with a limo and such."

Undecided on how much to tell her, Sebastian hesitated. It was a rather personal topic, and not the easiest thing for him to talk about. But then Brandi touched his wrist and when he looked at her, his entire body tightened.

"It's all right, Sebastian. I didn't mean to pry."

He went down without a whimper. He wanted to talk to her, to gain her trust. And this was as good a place to start as any. Leaning his head back against the soft leather upholstery of the seat, he said, "I grew up poor."

"I see."

He chuckled. "No, you don't. I'm not saying we couldn't afford a new car, I'm saying we barely afforded food. Half the time the electricity was turned off. Back then, hot water was a luxury, and in our neighborhood a peek at a limo would have been considered prime entertainment."

Brandi watched him, comprehension in her wide eyes. "So, wasting money still bothers you?"

"Bothers me? Yeah, it bothers me. I guess I learned to be especially thrifty—I had to, in order to make the food last. Now, even though money isn't an issue with me anymore, squandering it, even if it isn't mine... Well, it makes my stomach cramp. The only thing I've ever been extravagant with is my house. It gives me a kind of security I can't get anywhere else."

He waited for her reaction. He'd never before trusted a woman enough to share those personal thoughts. Admitting to such a weakness might have detracted from the image women had of him, and could have disillusioned anyone.

But Brandi didn't pull away. Instead, she took his hand, entwining her fingers with his. That one small gesture was so full of understanding, so full of giving that he was prompted to go on, knowing that *she* wouldn't be disillusioned by him or his truths. He wasn't certain why he knew that, but he did.

"My mother was incredible, trying so hard to make everything work. But she'd come home so exhausted from the extra hours at below minimum wage that she wouldn't even think of food. I tried to make certain she ate, but there were times when she was just too tired. There were also times when I couldn't find food to offer her."

"What about your father?"

He made a rude sound and Brandi squeezed his fingers. She was a tiny woman, half his size, but she had one hell of a grip—he felt it all the way to his heart.

"My father was a drunken, abusive bastard who only drank up what money my mother did make." He smiled, but it wasn't a nice smile. "He was the same type of man who keeps the women's shelters crowded. He wouldn't work to better his life. Hell, with the way he drank, he couldn't have kept a job even if he'd wanted to. So he was miserable. And rather than work toward fixing things, he'd turn around and...take out his anger on my mother.''

''He hit her?'' Brandi sounded appalled, but Sebastian had been pulled into his own memories, so he just shrugged. ''I can't even count the number of times I got woke up with my father cursing my mother and her crying. It would last for hours.''

Brandi sucked in a trembling breath and pulled away from him. He looked down at her, and froze. Her face shone pale in the dark interior of the car and her hands were fisted in her lap. She didn't look merely shocked—she looked livid. Without thinking, Sebastian said, ''Damn it, I'm sorry.'' And he tugged her close. She was stiff, resisting his comfort, but he needed it as much as she did so he didn't loosen his hold.

''I shouldn't have gone on like that. Hell, I don't even think about it all that much anymore, except for the waste of money. Brandi?'' He cradled her head between his palms and turned her face up to him. ''Are you okay?''

Nodding, she touched his cheek with a trembling hand. But her dark brows were still lowered and she looked almost ferocious. ''I'm sorry, Sebastian. You shouldn't have had to go through such an awful thing.''

"Me? It was my mother who had to put up with him."

She shook her head. "And you had to worry about both of them, didn't you?" She sniffed past her anger, a single tear glimmering in her eye.

Her reaction seemed extreme to him. Hell, it had happened long ago. He searched her face, but he saw no pity, no revulsion. There was only complete understanding, which confused him more than anything. How could a woman who'd come from a wonderful loving family really understand the coarse existence he had led?

Slowly, she pulled away from him and moved a few inches over on the seat, putting space between them. She gave him an uncertain look when he continued to watch her. "Do you ever see your father now?"

He made a sound, something between a choke and a snort. "Not a chance. Not when I was the one who chased him away."

"You?"

"When I was about twelve, I decided I'd had enough. I waited for my father with a chunk of broken lumber from the building site down the street. I considered it an equalizer. When he reached for my mother that last time, I stopped him."

"Extreme violence when necessary?" Her voice was a soft, gentling whisper.

He shrugged. "I took a few licks myself that day, but since my father had been disgustingly drunk, I doled out more than my fair share, too. And to a man like my father, it just wasn't worth hanging around if he had to take any abuse himself. He knew damn well, from that day on, he'd have to contend with me every time he showed up. So he left. And he never came back."

"But you saved your mother."

That was how Sebastian had consoled himself over the loss of his father, because despite everything, despite how absurd it seemed, he'd had feelings for the man. He had missed him when he'd just disappeared. For a while, it had been difficult, though those feelings had long since faded. "She never mentioned it, never said if she approved or disapproved. But she smiled more often after he'd gone. And knowing I'd managed to make a difference made me feel good too, even when I had an empty belly."

"My father is the most gentle man you'd ever meet," Brandi said softly. "He spoils us all, going overboard on gifts and affection. He can lecture a body crazy, but he'd never raise a hand against a woman in anger."

"You're lucky that your family is like that."

"I've always thought so." Then she said, "You must be very proud of all you've accomplished since then. You've overcome a very tragic background."

"Not all that tragic, and really, not all that different from what a lot of families live through. But it is what helped me decide on my future. And why I have such a successful business now."

"The personal protection agency?"

"Yes." Sebastian was astounded by how incredibly easy it was to talk to Brandi. Already, she knew more about him than most people did. "I decided I needed a job to help out after my father left, even though we were probably better off without buying his booze and with one less mouth to feed. I'd gained most of my height by then and I was street tough, so I hired myself out."

"You belonged to a gang?"

"I was my own gang." He chuckled now, remembering how full of himself he'd been. "I was a teenager, but I thought I was as capable as anyone. If someone needed protection, I supplied it. I was a big kid and I'd learned to be mean the hard way, by necessity. But I was choosy. I worked as a defense, not an offense. I wouldn't attack, only protect. And I made a bundle doing it."

"Sebastian…" She hesitated, but when he waited, she finally said, "It sounds like you learned how to live with the bad, not how to get away from it."

"True. It's called surviving. But I did finally figure that out, though not before a few scrapes with the law and a few near misses with my general well-being. Which is why I joined the service. College was out of the question. I barely made it through high school by the skin of my teeth. I wasn't dumb, just rebellious. And the service was structured enough to get me straightened out."

"It's incredible how you turned your life around."

Startled, he looked down to see Brandi watching him, her blue eyes wide and intense in the darkness, only an occasional streetlight glimmering across her features. His heart still aching with the memories of his painful childhood, he wanted nothing more than to kiss her, to take comfort and give it. But the moment his gaze dropped to her mouth, she stiffened, and once again he accepted the rejection.

This would probably be the longest five days of his life. Brandi didn't want him—might not ever want him—yet every minute with her, made him want her more. He felt an affinity with her that he'd never shared with another person. It didn't make sense, not with Brandi so petite and innocent and sweet—so much his opposite. Yet he felt it, because he felt her understanding, her concern, her giving....

Though he'd had lovers and female friends, none of them had affected him this way. Never had anyone gotten past his guard so effortlessly. Sharing so much time with her alone would be a unique form of torture.

He laughed off the discomfort. He really had no choice. "I'm incredible? Now you're starting to sound like Shay."

She grinned. "Heaven forbid."

When she continued to stare at him, her expression curious, he asked, "What?"

"You're such a...big man. I can't quite imagine you as a little kid. Do you look like your mother?"

"No. She was small, like you, but better rounded."

Brandi chuckled. "Shay is always telling me to eat more. But I could gain twenty pounds and still not be rounded, at least not in the right places."

"You're fine just the way you are. Tell Shay to mind her own business."

He'd said it in a teasing tone, but still Brandi looked embarrassed. "I'd like to meet your mother some day. I imagine she's very proud of you."

"She died years ago, Brandi. But my mother was always proud, even when I didn't deserve it. She used to claim I was the only good thing she had to look forward to. Which, when I look back to my misspent youth, is really pretty sad." Then he grinned, just so she wouldn't see how the topic affected him—how she affected him. "It's a parent's duty to be proud, no matter how you screw up."

In a voice so low he almost couldn't hear her, she said, "My parents haven't always been proud of me."

He stared at her profile, at her downcast expression, and frowned. "That can't be true. You've just said how your father dotes on you, and Shay brags about your mother all the time. They love you a lot."

"Yes, they do. But I've made some pretty terrible mistakes."

He wanted to know what kind of mistakes she was referring to. He couldn't imagine Brandi doing anything irresponsible or reckless. She didn't seem the type. But he also wanted her to confide in him freely. So he didn't ask. His job had taught him patience, especially with women, and he knew that if he bided his time, if he let her get to know him, she'd learn to be more comfortable with him.

She wouldn't look at him, and he had to cup her chin

to turn her face up to him. "We all make mistakes, honey. That's part of being human."

"I can't..." She hesitated, not another word forthcoming.

Sebastian gave her a small smile. "It's okay. No pressure, remember?"

She drew a deep breath, then blurted, "I shouldn't be here. You should have had this vacation with another woman. It was unfair of Shay to foist me off on you like this. But it's not too late. Maybe we could—"

"*Brandi.*" She went still as a stone, then blinked up at him. "I didn't want to be here with anyone else. I wanted to be here with you."

"But you don't understand."

"Understand what?" His temper frayed a bit and he struggled to control it. "That you're not interested in getting cozy with me? Believe me, I've figured that out already. And it's okay. I'm still enjoying your company."

"I fell asleep!"

"You were tired. I didn't mind."

"It was rude," she grumbled.

His sigh was long and loud. "Do you realize I've told you more about myself than any of my friends even know?" Her eyes widened. "I don't know why, damn it, I just felt like talking. You listened, so you've heard it all."

"I'm glad."

"And I'm glad you're here with me." He squeezed her shoulder. "We'll make the best of it, okay?"

She drew another deep breath, something she seemed to do when she was nervous, then let it out in a sigh. She peeked at him, her gaze hesitant. "I...I wanted to come. I really did."

"But?"

"I'm just not ready to do this."

He didn't know what *this* was, but several things came to mind. She might be in love with someone else. She might have had her heart broken, or maybe she wanted someone more influential, someone with her background. He didn't care. Whatever the obstacle, he'd overcome it somehow.

He'd been in his business long enough to know what appeared on the surface wasn't always the reality. Brandi seemed like such an enigma—bossy yet sweet, confident yet sometimes unsure. He had five days to learn more about her, to figure her out, and he was looking forward to every minute of it.

He smiled. "Are you forgetting you're in charge of this trip? We do what you want, when you want and how you want."

"I just...I don't like taking chances."

He didn't understand that, either, but it didn't matter, not at this moment. "I think you're ready to take a chance. A small chance," he added, just so she wouldn't stiffen up on him again. "With me."

"That's a rather arrogant assumption, isn't it?"

Of course it was, but he wouldn't admit it. "You know what I keep remembering, what I'll probably remember until I'm old and gray? The way you looked at me while I was on that damn stage. No woman has ever looked at me like that before. I liked it. A lot."

Just as he suspected, her spine snapped straight and her brows came down. But then the driver made a sudden sharp turn that threw her off balance and slammed her up against his side. Where she belonged.

Trying to ignore that vagrant observation, Sebastian slipped an arm around her and held her closer still. Before Brandi could slither away, the driver lowered the divider window. In serious tones meant to impress, he announced that they had arrived at the resort.

Sebastian grinned down at Brandi, seeing that she was flustered and embarrassed and, if he didn't miss his guess, a little excited by their close contact. "So, boss. Are you ready to take charge?"

She narrowed her eyes, not willing to give him the upper hand, even with his teasing. She lifted her small chin and treated him to her direct gaze. "I'm more than ready. I'm...anxious."

"Lord, help me." Sebastian felt his smile slip, but he covered his reaction quickly. "All right, then. Let the vacation begin."

4

SEBASTIAN COULD TELL Brandi loved the opulence of the "cabin" they'd been directed to. But he felt almost rigid with uneasiness. It appeared to be a damn honeymoon retreat, sinfully extravagant and seductive.

The limo had dropped them off at the main lodge where they'd been preregistered. The desk clerk gave them a key and a flashlight then pointed them to a narrow trail that led through the woods, explaining that their luggage would be brought around shortly. A rental car was at their disposal, but wasn't needed to reach the cabin.

Sebastian had held her hand as they walked through the darkened wood, the flashlight beam bouncing off thick trees and rocks. Brandi hadn't said a word. She'd been quiet, introspective, her fingers cold in his grip. But as soon as the cabin came into sight, he'd felt her enthusiasm.

He didn't want to dampen that enthusiasm. It was the first time he'd seen her so excited, and she looked beautiful, her smile wide, her eyes bright in the darkness. Even her wild curls seemed to bounce with energy.

How anyone could call the small rustic house a cabin

was beyond him. Set off alone in the woods, it provided picturesque privacy. A floodlight had been left on in front and Sebastian could see an angular deck filled with lavish, well-padded patio furniture. The front room had a skylight over the entrance door and rough quarry stone for a fireplace filled the adjacent outside wall.

With Brandi practically dancing beside him, he had no choice but to unlock the door and step inside.

"It's perfect!"

"It's too much." His grim tone must have reached her, because she swatted his arm.

"None of that now. I know how you must feel, but let's try to enjoy ourselves, all right? After all, Shay went to all this trouble."

But to what end? Without an ounce of subtlety, Shay had dropped them into a honeymoon suite, that's what she'd done. Sebastian kept the thought to himself. Brandi was still skittish with him and he didn't want to damage the fragile bond they'd forged. But how in hell was he supposed to survive this? Every male hormone in his body had been on red alert since he'd first seen her. The ambiance of the damn cabin would only heighten the feeling.

Brandi had already hustled off, peeking into every room and inspecting every corner. "There's a water bed in one of the bedrooms, with a private bath!"

Sebastian was still looking around the front room, but despite himself, her awe brought on a small smile. It had been a long time since he'd been able to feel any passion over needlessly blowing money. With Brandi, all he *did* feel was passion. "Why don't you use that room?"

She stuck her head out the doorway and grinned at him. "I think I will, but only because the other bedroom has a king-size bed." Her gaze dipped over his long frame and she cocked one eyebrow. "That'll suit you just fine, I'm sure."

She disappeared again, this time through the kitchen and after a moment, he heard, "There's a hot tub in the back on an enclosed deck!"

Erotic thoughts and images of warm water and nude female flesh—Brandi's flesh—immediately came to mind. Sebastian had to swallow, and even then, his voice sounded uneven...and very hopeful. "Would you like to unpack and try it out?"

Silence. Brandi came slinking back through the kitchen with her head down and her hands gripped together at her waist. "Um, not tonight. It's late and I'm really tired."

She didn't look at him. Sebastian watched her wrestle with her indecision then finally pry her hands apart in an effort to relax. With a sigh of resignation, he accepted that the Jacuzzi was out for a while. "Maybe tomorrow, then." He stretched, trying to unknot his own muscles with Brandi watching his every move. She jumped when a knock sounded at the door.

"Our luggage." Opening his wallet to retrieve a tip, he said over his shoulder, "Why don't you see what the kitchen has in stock while I carry in our bags? I could use a bite to eat."

But after he'd put the last piece of luggage in the bedrooms—trying his best not to look at the bed Brandi would sleep in—he found her reading a room service menu that had been left on the small dining table. Frowning, he asked, "The kitchen's not stocked?"

Brandi waved a hand. "There's food in there. But I don't feel like cooking. Let's just order something."

He took the menu from her hand and then whistled at the prices. "You've got to be kidding. I could eat a week off what they charge. Besides, it's after midnight. Do you really think they'll serve this late?"

"Well, maybe not. But if it's the money, I can..."

"No. Absolutely not." Appalled by what she'd been about to suggest, Sebastian added, "I can damn well afford it if we decide to order in. It just seems ridiculous to pay those prices if there's food here."

"But cooking is so much trouble. And as you said, it's after midnight."

Without really meaning to, he touched a knuckle to her soft, warm cheek. "You do look exhausted. Why don't you go get ready for bed and I'll get the food together?"

It was probably to escape his touch as much from weariness that she agreed so quickly. "If you're sure you don't mind."

She was already on her feet and heading out, so he chuckled. "I don't mind at all."

He wanted her to leave, before she noticed how she

affected him. He was half-hard just thinking of her getting ready for bed, wondering what she'd wear, if she'd shower first.

He heard the water pipes hum and had his answer. It took him several moments before he could get his feet to move, and then he went to rummage in the kitchen cabinets. He found canned soup and crackers and cheese. He also found champagne and knew Shay had struck once again. He would definitely have to speak to her about this propensity she had for wasting money.

After putting the soup on to simmer and slicing a few chunks of cheese, he went back to the living room to start a fire. The cabin was set up in an airy, open way. The living room, tiny dining room and kitchen were all open to each other with two bedrooms at the back of the house. Brandi's bedroom had its own bath, with another full bath at the end of the hall between the rooms.

The ceilings were cathedral with raw wood beams, the floors polished pine with scattered handwoven rugs. A thick cushioned couch and two matching chairs faced the fireplace on one wall, the entertainment center on the other. Ignoring the television and VCR, Sebastian turned on the stereo and found a soft music station.

There was wood already laid in the fireplace and he had a fire blazing in no time. It took the small nip out of the late spring air and added a certain ambiance that belonged in the cabin. The darkness outside was endless. With the floodlights turned off, not even the woods were visible. Inside, the smell of soup and wood smoke scented the air. It was as if they were sealed in together, isolated from the rest of the world, intimate.

He found himself appreciating the cabin, rather than resenting it, because it afforded him the time alone with Brandi that he needed.

Already his stomach was knotting at the thought of the night to come. He would be alone with a woman he wanted more than he could ever recall wanting anyone or anything, yet she froze at his every touch. He had to find a way to breach her reserve, but he didn't know how. One minute she seemed interested, the next repelled. Somehow both reactions only increased his determination to reach her.

When he stood and brushed off his hands, his peripheral vision caught a smidge of white and he turned.

Brandi stood there, looking uncertain and damp and so incredibly sexy he couldn't help but react. If she'd been any other woman, he'd have gone to her, picked her up and carried into the nearest bedroom. He could have spent hours making love to her, alternating between the tenderness she instilled and the hot, primal urges that kept surging through him. He could envision their lovemaking as wild and hard, but also sweet and easy. Either way would do a lot toward satisfying the gnawing need in his gut.

But this was Brandi, and he wanted some kind of

emotional commitment from her as much as the physical release. It had never mattered to him before, but then, he'd never met anyone like her. Somehow with her sweetness and caring, she'd gotten under his skin, and the thought of sex without emotion wasn't appealing.

He wanted her. All of her.

He had five days, so he'd be patient—no matter how his body rebelled at the thought. He was a tactician, one of the best. His skill had been honed in the service and on his job. He could ruthlessly plan her surrender with great skill, and she wouldn't know what was happening until it was too late.

But for now, if she noticed the force of his erection and the taut way he barely managed to hold on to his control, she'd find a fast plane back to Jackson.

He cleared his throat. "The soup should be ready in just a minute."

She fidgeted with the belt to her thick white robe. It shouldn't have looked so damn sexy, but it did. Terry cloth covered her from her neck, where she had the lapels folded over so not a hint of skin showed, to the tops of her bare feet. He had no idea what she wore underneath, and that fact almost made him crazy.

She'd washed her hair. The damp curls weren't quite as unruly as before, but somehow, with the small curls clinging to her cheeks and forehead, she looked even more enticing. She'd belted the robe tightly and he could see how tiny her waist was, but other than that, not a single curve showed through the thick material.

She still hadn't said anything and he stumbled through more awkward conversation.

"You should have something on your feet. It's a little chilly in here."

"There weren't any slippers in my luggage. Whoever packed must have forgotten."

Her voice sounded strained, breathless, and he stared again, unable to help himself.

"Sebastian?"

"I'll get you a pair of my socks." He left the room, knowing if he stood there a second longer, he'd give himself away. Not even Brandi could have missed the way the material of his khaki slacks strained over his zipper. No female had ever had such a profound effect on him. He felt as though he'd been involved in heavy foreplay for an hour. And all she'd done was change into a robe. A robe for bed. A water bed.

He rubbed the back of his neck and cursed.

When he came back with the socks, his libido somewhat under control, Brandi was stirring the soup. He watched for a moment, appreciating the way her hips moved in cadence with her hand. Barbarian that he admittedly was, he found something intrinsically appealing at the sight of a woman in her bathrobe, barefoot, at the stove. He grinned at the thought. The female population of Jackson would string him up if they could read his mind right then.

Almost in silence, he handed her the socks and while she tugged them on he found a tray. He poured the soup into bowls, added the crackers and cheese while

Brandi found two sodas in the fridge. He was grateful she'd ignored the champagne.

They carried the whole thing into the living room. Brandi settled herself on the floor in front of the fire, so Sebastian did the same. He was content just to watch her, the way she tucked her slim legs beneath her, how she fluffed her drying hair. She seemed very introspective, her thoughts deep as she started on her soup without comment. After a few minutes, she looked at him.

"This is great. Thanks. Much better than waiting on room service."

Sebastian only nodded, so turned on he couldn't think of a reply. Soon he'd be demented with lust, he thought.

She bit her lip, then went on. "I've never done this before. I'm sorry if I'm not being very good company." Her cheeks turned red and she bit her lip again. "I...I have no idea what we're supposed to talk about."

"We don't have to talk about anything." Ignoring his strangled tone, he set his nearly empty soup bowl aside. "Brandi, I want you to be comfortable, remember? You're calling the shots this trip. If you want to just sit quietly, that's fine."

She too set her bowl back on the tray. "It's not that. I mean, I want to talk to you. But...have you ever done this before?"

"This?" His heartbeat picked up rhythm, pumping warm blood to places that already felt too full.

"You know. Sitting alone with a woman in a private

place. Eating in front of the fire. Struggling for conversation."

"With the woman in her bedclothes? No, I've never done this before. At least, not when we planned to go to two separate bedrooms. This cabin..."

"I know you don't like it."

"I like it fine. It's just that it's meant as a lover's retreat." He didn't mention the amount of money it probably cost. That issue was secondary to how he felt right now.

He tried to see her face, to read her eyes, but she kept her gaze averted. "Brandi, I can't pretend I don't want you." His low, husky tone grabbed her full attention. Her head swung around, her expression bordering on shock.

"Damn it." Sebastian stood, then paced a few feet away. When he turned to Brandi again, she looked...almost fearful. He dropped to his knees beside her and tried to ignore the way she cowered back from him. "I'm sorry. Honey, you have to know how difficult this is for me. You don't seem to realize it, but you're a very sexy woman."

"I am not!"

"Yes, you are." He smiled now, some of his frustration giving way to amusement. "And here we are alone, in this love pit."

She raised her brows and a smile hovered on her lips as she, too, started to relax. "Love pit?"

"The water bed? The Jacuzzi? The fireplace? This cabin is meant to seduce. Only I know that's not what you want. And I gave you my word not to pressure you."

"And you always keep your word?" When he nodded, she asked, "I'm the one in charge, right?"

He swallowed, not certain where she was going with her reasoning, but he had a few hopeful ideas. So did his body. "Absolutely."

Her cheeks heated more, and once again her small teeth sank into her bottom lip while she peeked up at him. He wanted those sharp white teeth on him, wanted to soothe her lips himself. Then finally she straightened and looked determined. His thighs tightened in expectation. "All right. I'm in charge. And right now, I think I'd like a kiss."

After making that bold statement, which seemed to take all her nerve, she lowered her lashes and whispered, "That is, if you wouldn't mind? I mean, I know that probably wasn't part of your original agreement, but..."

Sebastian's brain felt like mush but his body was granite hard. He wasn't at all sure he'd heard her right. "A kiss?"

"If you would."

He would all right. Gladly. Even if it killed him, which it just might because a kiss was a far cry from what he wanted, from what he needed right now.

Watching her face for any sign of retreat, he whispered, "There's kisses, and then there's kisses. The kind you want may not be the kind I'm wanting to give you. Why don't you be more specific so I don't screw this up?"

With her fingertip, Brandi drew an idle design over the rug. She peeked up at him, then away again. "Why don't you just start with the one you think I want...then maybe we can try the one you want to give me?"

BRANDI WAITED, holding her breath, while Sebastian apparently considered her suggestion. He scooted closer and her heartbeat raced with a mixture of dread and excitement. She really wanted to enjoy his kiss and, so far, the only fear she felt was that she might make a fool of herself. The possibility always existed, and she didn't think she could bear it if—

His fingertips touched her jaw, suspending all thought. Gently, he tipped up her chin and her vision was filled by him, the heat in his gaze, the tautness of his expression. Gentleness seemed a part of him, incongruous with his obvious strength, his massive size. The contrasts had intrigued her from the start. She could easily picture him defending a person with lethal skill, then soothing that person with his quiet, sure manner.

It was almost impossible not to trust him, because his power was tempered by genuine caring. All his life, he'd been taking care of others. Brandi wanted to take care of him. She just wasn't sure she knew how.

His eyes closed and hers closed as well as she waited breathlessly for his kiss. Then she felt it, the brief, heated touch of his mouth on her own. His breath fanned her cheek, and his lips moved the smallest bit, coasting over hers, teasing.

She wanted to touch him, to put her hands on that broad hard chest, but she was afraid. Afraid of failure, afraid of how he might react. Afraid of how she might react.

Slowly he pulled away, just enough to put space between them but not enough that she couldn't feel him, his nearness, his heat. Her eyes opened and she saw him watching her, his gaze intent and probing. She swallowed. Her heartbeat knocked against her ribs and there was a queer little tingle in the pit of her stomach, stirred by his hot musky scent. She started to speak, but he laid a finger over her lips.

"That was the kiss you wanted."

Feeling numb, Brandi nodded.

"Do you want to go on?"

It was the sound of his voice that decided her. Rough and grating, like a man on the edge of control. She licked her lips and accidently touched his finger. His expression hardened even more, and before she could deny him, before she had to stumble her way though an explanation she couldn't give, he pulled back.

"No. I don't think we should play this game any more. At least not right now. You might be ready for it, but I don't think I am."

His comment about games distracted her from her worries, so that even though he'd given her an out, she said, "I thought it was my decision to make. I'm the one in charge, remember?"

"I have no intention of forgetting." Then his thick dark lashes lowered and he looked at her through slumberous eyes. "In fact, since you're the one in charge, why don't you do the kissing? Then we'll both know for certain that you're getting exactly what you want."

The idea fascinated her. Sebastian leaned back until his shoulders were braced against the sofa. He stretched out his long muscled legs and crossed his ankles, then folded his arms over his chest. He looked negligent and at his ease—not in any way a threat. Except for his eyes. They shone with heat, the green bright and excited. But instead of fear, Brandi was suffused by her first dose of feminine power.

Rising to her knees, she said, "Don't move."

His jaw hardened, but he nodded. His eyes never left her.

She inched closer, watching him, but he remained in his contained pose. Carefully she placed her palms on his shoulders. He felt so hard, like warm, smooth stone. The muscles bunched beneath her fingers and she dug in just a little, like a cat testing the texture of his body, but there was almost no resilience here. The man was simply hard all over.

He made a small sound, but stayed completely still. Brandi stared at his mouth. The slight growth of whiskers there looked sexy to her, and she wanted to touch his skin, to taste him and luxuriate in his scent. She hadn't known a man could smell so delicious. Instead, feeling like a coward, she leaned down and placed a hard, quick peck on his mouth, then looked to see his reaction.

"That isn't what you wanted, Brandi. Is it?"

Oh, that husky voice, thick with desire, challenging her. Shivering with reaction, she leaned down again. This time she let her mouth linger, each move calculated. Until she forgot what she was doing, until the heady scent of him filled her and she felt drunk and anxious and hot. His tongue came out to glide along her bottom lip and he made a rough sound of pleasure. Brandi gasped. He used that second to lick inside her lips, to explore the edge of her teeth. He kept his hands and body still. Nothing moved except for his mouth, which now slanted against hers.

Brandi leaned a little more heavily into him and he groaned.

Just that quickly, she remembered herself and jerked away. Good grief, she hadn't meant for things to go so far. She'd only wanted to try a simple kiss. But when she saw how dark Sebastian's cheeks had become, how hard his jaw looked, the fierce green of his eyes, she knew she'd gone too far.

She came to her feet in a rush. Still he didn't move, he only watched her. And waited. "I'm sorry. I...I should go on to bed now."

With his arms still crossed over his chest, he slowly nodded. In a slow, deep whisper, he said, "Good night, Brandi."

"I..." She wanted to explain, to try to make him understand.

With a leisurely thoroughness that had her stomach doing flips, his gaze moved over her, and he said, "It's all right. You don't have to say anything."

He shifted slightly, uncrossing his ankles and parting them just a bit. Her gaze was drawn downward. She couldn't miss the sight of his bold erection, pressing taut against his slacks. That part of him looked huge and hard, in concordance with the rest of his big body. Heat washed over her, both from embarrassment and excitement. It seemed impossible to breathe, looking at the length of him, his size. Her lips parted, but no words came out.

She could hear the masculine amusement in his next words. "Like I said, you're a very sexy lady. And I'm not exactly immune."

Brandi gulped. "Good night, Sebastian."

She rushed from the room, but when she peeked back over her shoulder at him, it was to see his head dropped back on the cushions of the couch, one forearm over his eyes. He looked like a man in pain. Or in desperate need.

She didn't like herself for it, but a small kernel of satisfaction swelled inside her. A man like Sebastian...and he wanted her. She had kissed him. She had touched him. She was on her way to a full recovery.

Maybe this vacation wouldn't be so bad after all.

"DO YOU HAVE to buy every damn thing you see?"

Brandi tried to hide her grin as she listened to Sebastian's continual grumping. She'd slept like the dead last night, content with her progress, with her new experimentation. But evidently Sebastian hadn't slept much at all. He looked tired today and his mood could only be described as grouchy.

"You don't like the horse? I think he's kind of cute."

"The damn thing looks ridiculous. The head is too big, and the color is ludicrous. You paid way too much for it."

"It's a souvenir. Of course it cost more than it should."

He made a sound of exasperation, then eyed her shopping bag. "At the marina this morning you bought fake fish, then at the breakfast inn you bought two milkmaid dolls."

"Two very cute milkmaid dolls," she corrected. "And I've had a great time today, Sebastian. Even though it was still a little cold on the lake this morning, I enjoyed the rowboat. I couldn't believe what horrible beggars those big carp were." She knew her gratitude would only annoy him more. Each and every time she thanked him, he frowned.

"This is supposed to be your vacation, Brandi. You're supposed to have a good time."

"And I am. Especially with the shopping." It was the truth, but she had an ulterior motive, also. Since Sebastian was helping her without even realizing it, she wanted to help him, too. She hoped to get him to loosen up a little about money. Like Sebastian, she didn't believe in squandering her cash, but neither did she enjoy putting herself on a shoestring budget, not when she could afford better. Sebastian simply wasn't used to putting his own needs and desires first; his life centered around helping others. It was past time he gave himself some happiness.

"What the hell are you going to do with all that junk, anyway?"

It hadn't been easy, but Brandi had managed to convince him to go shopping along the main strip with her after breakfast. She'd been forced to resort to coercion, reminding him that she was in charge. He'd given in with little grace, and now they'd been at it for hours, not even stopping for lunch.

She'd hoped he'd get into the spirit of it, but obviously the man did not like to shop. He had no appreciation for the many quaint little speciality stores. Brandi, on the other hand, had bought something from almost every shop.

It had rained first thing in the morning, but now the sun was out and shining brightly and the day seemed beautiful to her, though it still wasn't overly warm. She was comfortable in a long denim skirt and loose navy blue sweater. Sebastian wore jeans and another polo shirt, this one dark gray. He looked very handsome, if a bit surly.

Still, even with his attitude turned sour, he was a perfect gentleman. Every time she left a shop, Sebastian took her hand. He protected her from the flow of human traffic and steered her around mud puddles. It felt right to have him so close, to feel his warmth and strength.

"If you must know, I want to take a gift back to each of the kids at the shelter. They get so few presents."

She said it carelessly, but still he looked dumbstruck, then shamefaced. "Damn it. I'm sorry." He rubbed his eyes with his free hand, then sighed. "I know I'm being a bastard today, but I didn't get much sleep last night. How 'bout a cup of coffee? The caffeine will do me good, and your feet have got to be getting tired."

Actually, she felt fine, but he looked ready to drop, so she took mercy on him. "I only have two more gifts to buy. Why don't you go for your coffee and I'll meet you there in a few minutes."

His hand tightened on hers. "I can go with you. I should probably pick up something for the kids, too. I just hadn't thought about it."

Her heart softened and the urge to hug him close almost overwhelmed her. "It's not necessary, Sebastian. I already have plenty of gifts." He didn't look convinced, so she added, "Look, right there on the corner is a café. I'll hit this last shop, grab a few more gifts and then join you. Give me fifteen minutes."

He still hesitated, probably because she tended to spend closer to forty-five minutes in each shop, but she gave him a look of insistence. "Go. I order you. And I'm the boss remember? Guzzle coffee. Wake yourself up."

Finally he nodded and turned away. She watched until he'd crossed the street and disappeared into the crowd. This vacation was turning out to be a revelation. For such a long time, she'd hidden behind her independence and privacy, never wanting anyone to invade her space, to get too close and ponder her thoughts. But now, she already missed having Sebastian at her side.

It filled her with warmth to think of him, which she did. The whole time she considered small collectibles from the souvenir shop, part of her mind was on Sebastian. Their kiss last night had probably not meant much to him, but to her it had been an accomplishment, a giant step forward. Not since she was eighteen had she kissed a man, or even wanted to. The thought had been nothing less than repellent, the memories stored with it, horrifying. But there was nothing repellent about Sebastian Sinclair. The man could make her tremble with just a look.

With her mind half on her newest purchases, and half on getting back to Sebastian, it was no wonder she almost ran into the men. When she finally did see them, it was too late to step out of their way. Within a second, the two of them had crowded her into the store's brick front.

Brandi felt the visceral panic swell, but she fought it back. They were on a busy street. No harm could come to her. Still, as one of the men gave a long, low whistle, she jerked back, memories assailing her. Both men laughed.

One of them gave her a genuine smile. "You look like you could use some help with that big shopping bag, honey. Why don't I give you a lift to wherever

you're going? Or better yet, to where we're going.
What do you say?"

She tried to answer, but no words would come, not
even a denial. The men were too close, towering over
her.

The other one stepped closer still. "She doesn't want
you, Josh. Why not give me a chance?" Then he gave
her a wide grin. "How about it, sweetheart? You up for
a little fun?"

She shook her head, hating her cowardice, the gnawing fear. The first man frowned, looking concerned and
he reached for her. She bolted. Feeling foolish even as
her legs stretched out, she raced toward the street, her
shopping bag clutched to her middle. She heard the
men give a surprised burst of laughter at her mad
dash, and tears stung her eyes. Frantically, she
searched for Sebastian, but didn't see him, which made
the panic even worse.

When someone took her arm from behind, she
started to scream, but the sound was cut off as she was
whipped around and both arms grabbed in a tight
hold. "What the hell is the matter with you? What's
happened?"

Sebastian. Brandi threw herself against his familiar
strength, uncaring that they were drawing notice, or
that he might feel her violent trembling. She clung tight
to him as she tried to shake the fear. Rather than asking
questions, he held her close until she calmed. Several
minutes passed in complete silence except for her rac-
ing breaths. Sebastian's big hands smoothed up and

down her back, and twice she felt the light touch of a kiss to her temple. When she lifted her face from his chest, he surveyed her, then with a grim look, said, "Come on," and started them down the street, his arm tight around her waist. She went with him gladly, not even protesting when he pried her shopping bag out of her numb fingers to carry it for her.

Taking them slightly off the main drag, he urged her toward a low stone fence and then lifted her up to sit. Pink-and-white azaleas bloomed all around them, their sweet scent heady in the air. Sebastian stood in front of her, his legs braced apart, his expression enigmatic. "Tell me what happened, Brandi."

Oh, God, she couldn't. She closed her eyes and shook her head. Sebastian stepped forward until her knees brushed against the front of his body. She didn't dare look down to see exactly where they touched.

"Brandi, you're as pale a ghost."

"And every bit as vapid," she said in disgust.

"You want to tell me what that means?"

"Not particularly." She'd acted the fool, once again. She might as well have been eighteen again, the fear had come back that strong. She was ridiculous and stupid and...

"Brandi? Talk to me, honey, right now. I don't like this one damn bit."

She could hear the genuine concern in his words. Reaching out, she took his hands and held them. "I'm sorry. I overreacted, that's all. Sometimes I can be very silly and foolish."

"Overreacted to what?"

Uh-oh. He sounded ready to do bodily harm to someone. Eight years of military training and hardness sounded in his tone. The barbarian warrior was back.

But no real harm had been done. The men hadn't even been all that brazen. "It's nothing, really. Two men got a little friendly, that's all. And I...well, it frightened me just a bit. I behaved like an idiot, running off like I did."

He didn't look convinced, but he did correct her. "You didn't run off. You ran to me."

"Well...yeah, I guess I did."

"You felt safer with me."

"I know you, for crying out loud! I didn't know these men. Don't make more of it than it is."

"What did they say to you?"

Now that she was away from them and the panic had ebbed, she couldn't bear to repeat it all. "They were just two men flirting the way men do. They said a few things, and I should have answered them, to put them in their place. But instead, I just ran off."

"To me."

Brandi rolled her eyes. He did seem to be stuck on that small fact. "Yes, to you. Did you expect me to run all the way back to the cabin?"

"I didn't expect you to be running at all or I never would have left you alone. It didn't feel right in the first place. I was just coming to get you when I saw you dashing across the street."

Needing desperately to change the subject, she asked, "Did you get your coffee?"

"No. I saw a sign for an outdoor musical and thought that would work as good as caffeine to wake me up. You want to go? We could grab a hamburger or something there for dinner."

Surprised, Brandi checked her watch. It was going on five o'clock. The morning and afternoon had flown by and they hadn't eaten since breakfast. The idea of an outdoor concert was appealing, but she preferred the privacy of the cabin for dinner. "We can check out the concert, but there's no way I'm going to eat a greasy hamburger. I want real food tonight."

"Fair enough. How about an hour or so of music, then you can pick the restaurant we eat at?"

"No restaurant. I want to go back to the cabin and order room service."

At first, Sebastian didn't answer her. Brandi knew how he felt about the expensive meals the lodge offered, but she needed some privacy tonight, away from the crowds. And she wanted to teach him to take pleasure in the small things, even when they cost a bit more. She half expected an argument from him, especially given his earlier contentious mood. But then he took a deep breath and asked, "Did anyone pack you a swimsuit?"

"I think so. Why?"

"Yesterday you showed some interest in the Jacuzzi." His gaze dropped to her mouth and stayed there. "I thought maybe after dinner you'd want to try it out. It might help to relax you."

Heat uncurled, chasing away the last remnants of embarrassment over her flight of terror. "Do you have a swimsuit?"

"No. But I can just wear my briefs." His gaze held hers, his eyes bright. "As long as you don't have a problem with it."

Brandi knew in that instant exactly where her knees touched him. She felt his body stir, felt his erection grow hard and long, and knew it was the thought of being with her that affected him so strongly. But she was in charge. She could do this—play in the Jacuzzi, indulge in the special feeling of being alone with him—with no fear of being pushed and no fear of consequences.

She called all the shots, and she trusted him to abide by her rules.

Knowing he expected her to refuse, or to at least look shocked, she lifted her chin and nodded. "All right. We can try out the Jacuzzi. But dinner first."

Though his expression didn't change, she saw him draw a deep breath. He lifted her from the wall, then stood there looking down at her. "What the hell? I think I'll need to restore my energy with a good meal anyway."

5

WAITING THROUGH the concert had just about killed him.

Sitting in the grass with Brandi at his side, her body swaying in time to the music, was enough to make him crazy. But what played even more havoc with his male libido was the memory of how she'd run to him. Whatever had frightened her—and he had no doubt there was more to it than she claimed—she'd run to him. Even though she hadn't trusted him enough to share the whole truth, it still had to be counted as progress. No wonder his mood was uncertain today. She kept throwing him off balance. It had all started with that kiss last night, a sweet little kiss that had kept him awake tossing and turning until the early morning. Since then he hadn't been able to get his thoughts gathered.

Something had happened during that brief, all too innocent kiss. And it had to do with Brandi taking control. He'd suggested it as lark, hoping to encourage her. But it had gone beyond that. Somehow, they'd crossed some invisible boundary. He only wished he knew what it was.

Waiting through the concert had been torture

enough, but compared to that, dinner was the Spanish Inquisition. He hadn't even found the wit to complain about the damn T-bone steaks Brandi ordered, steaks that had cost enough to feed a family of four. When she finally leaned back in her seat and pronounced herself finished, he pushed away the rest of his uneaten steak and offered to do the dishes.

She shyly looked away. "No, you did the dishes last night after I went to bed. It's my turn."

He'd taken care of cleaning up and banking the fire just to give himself something to do. But it hadn't worked. He'd still wanted her so much sleep wouldn't come. All because of that one simple but explosive kiss.

He didn't argue with her now, not when he had other things to accomplish. "Fine. You can do the dishes and I'll go take the cover off the Jacuzzi."

Brandi came to her feet, wringing her hands. "You don't think anyone could see us out there, do you?"

"This cabin's pretty isolated. And there's no one around, but we can leave the lights off if you want."

"No!" She blinked, then collected her control. "That is, I like the lights on. Maybe just a few dim ones."

More secrets for him to try to decipher. But he could be patient when the end result was worth it, and this was definitely worth it. "I saw some candles in the cupboard. Will candlelight do?"

Nodding, she whispered, "Yes, that would be fine. Thank you."

He smiled at her formality, then couldn't help but touch her. His fingers drifted over her cheek, then catching one curl and tugging lightly. "Hurry and change into your suit. I'll wait for you in the Jacuzzi."

She looked relieved that she wouldn't have to face him under the bright fluorescent lighting of the kitchen. The truth was, he'd been thinking of himself. Already, his body was anxious for the sight of her. Being in the water was more to preserve his modesty than hers.

He grabbed three fat candles from the shelf and a pack of matches. Brandi already had the two dishes scraped and returned to the basket they'd come in. All she had to do was place them back on the front porch to be picked up later. She glanced at Sebastian, her blue eyes dark with uncertainty, then smiled and left the kitchen. He went outside to get things set up.

And hopefully to get himself under control.

Fifteen minutes later, while he impatiently waited for Brandi, he realized no amount of warm churning water could ease him. His muscles felt restricted and he hummed with tension. His breathing was thick, his arousal complete. All it would take would be one small smile from her and he'd be a goner. He tilted his head back and stared up at the stars through the glass roof of the enclosed patio. Muted candlelight flickered around the deck, casting a warm mellow glow over the water...over him. But he was far from mellow.

He should have given in and taken care of his need last night. Lying in his bed, he'd given it serious thought. But finding satisfaction without Brandi hadn't seemed right. He didn't want to revert back to the tactics of his youth. He wanted Brandi—over him, under him—any way at all.

He heard a soft sound and his body hardened even more. He was so painfully erect, he hurt. The caress of the bubbling water only served to arouse him more, not ease him. Slowly, he shifted his gaze from the stars to the deck, searching out Brandi's slight silhouette. She stood facing the Jacuzzi, her body curiously still, feet together, hands at her sides. Her skin shone white against the darkness of the early evening sky and the black of her one-piece swimsuit. She was so tiny, so female. Her curves weren't voluptuous, but they were there, and all the more enticing for being so subtle. Her hips were narrow, only slightly rounded, her legs slim. He saw her tremble and he gave her a smile.

He didn't say a word, only held out a hand. After a long hesitation, Brandi took it. Once she'd stepped down into the water, she released his hand and moved away from him to the other side of the tub. She slowly sank into the warm water, finding the bench that circled the tub. He heard her soft sigh as the heat enveloped her.

Silence dragged on, then Sebastian levered himself up and over to her. Without asking, he positioned himself close beside her. The water sloshed around them before settling into a froth again. Brandi glanced up at him, then whispered, "Sebastian?"

"I'd like to kiss you again." The rough, aroused gravel of his voice didn't embarrass him. He wanted her, and he didn't mind her knowing it.

Brandi dragged her fingers through the water, not looking at him. "I kissed you, remember?"

He smiled, though it pained him to do so. "Will you kiss me again?"

"Will you move?"

Frowning, he asked, "You want me to move away from you?" He didn't understand her, but he wanted to. And this was her show. Much as he'd have liked to call the shots, he was leaving it all up to her.

She still hadn't looked at him, but he caught her chin and lifted her face. "Talk to me, honey. If you don't tell me what you want, what you need, then I can't know. And I want to make you happy."

He felt her sigh, felt her scoot a few inches away from him. The candles afforded enough light for him to see her face, her eyes wide, her lips slightly parted. She looked uneasy, undecided. "Brandi?"

"I want to kiss you," she whispered, her low voice filled with embarrassment...and maybe some excitement. "But I don't want you to touch me."

He searched her face, trying to glean the meaning behind her words. Maybe she was just into control. If she wanted to play sex games, he was more than willing. But he had to know the rules.

When he remained silent, she pulled farther away from him. "Never mind. I'm sorry."

"No, wait." He caught her arm, felt her stiffen and immediately released her. "Just spell it out for me, okay? I don't mind playing."

Now she looked confused, but after several deep

breaths, she muttered, "Remember how you sat last night? When I...I kissed you?"

He settled lower on the bench beneath the water's level, resting on his spine. He crossed his arms over his chest and looked at her. "Like this?"

"Yes." She half turned to face him, coming up some on her knees. "Just like that. Now don't move."

His jaw clenched. He didn't know if he could take it. The black suit clung to her small breasts and narrow ribs. Her shoulders gleamed with moisture, the curls in her hair were already damp from the steam. His body throbbed in anticipation as she leaned toward him. He didn't dare close his eyes; never had a kiss meant as much as this one.

Her right breast touched his shoulder and he could feel her stiff little nipple poking at him, making him shudder. He wanted to touch that nipple with his fingertips, tease it with his teeth and tongue, suck her deep into his mouth.

His breathing became choppy, and even though he felt foolish, he couldn't help the instinctive response to her nearness. Her breath fanned his cheek, then his lips and then finally she kissed him.

His groan erupted despite his efforts to remain quiet. But he didn't move. It was a measure of his control that he restrained himself. The touch of her mouth was inquisitive, cautious. He needed so badly to haul her close, to turn her so he could press over her, feel her breasts burning against his chest, feel the part of her slender thighs to cradle his erection.

But he remained immobile, only his panting breaths giving away his excitement. She leaned back.

"Sebastian? Are you okay?"

He half laughed, half groaned. "I'm so damn hot, it's a wonder this water isn't boiling." He bit back the need to touch her and said instead, "You have no idea how much I want you, do you? How close I am to exploding."

Her gaze searched his face, and he saw her incomprehension.

"Brandi, I'm a touch away from coming right here in the damn water. And right now, I'd give just about anything for that touch."

"Oh." Her gaze dropped to the churning surface of the water, searching.

He managed another laugh, husky and deep and persuasive. "You can't see what I mean—but you could feel."

Before he'd finished, she was shaking her head. "No, I can't."

"Why not? You're in charge. You can do whatever you want." He added in a soft promise, "I'm not going to move."

She wanted to. He could tell by her unsteady breathing, by the way she stared at him as if trying to come to a decision. He didn't dare move, afraid she'd choose to leave him. He waited, and it felt like a lifetime before her gaze dropped again and he saw her hand dip into the water.

His body vibrated with a deep groan—a response in

anticipation to her touch. Her fingertips bumped against his hard thigh, then shyly slid higher to the smoother skin of his hip. His thighs parted the slightest bit; her hand moved to the inside of his knee.

He knew he was working on a hair trigger. It was no longer a matter of exquisite torture—he had lost his control.

Sebastian jerked away, unwilling to embarrass her, unwilling to be pushed so far over the edge. It was insanity the way she affected him. This wasn't the time or place. He couldn't rush things, not until Brandi was ready to be with him every step of the way. Whatever game she wanted to play, she'd have to play it when he was in better control.

"I thought..."

Her voice quavered, and his irritation with himself grew. "Forget it," he rumbled, "I'm sorry, but the game is over."

He heard a splash and turned just in time to catch Brandi's arm. She crouched on the edge of the Jacuzzi, her face white, her eyes wide, almost wild. "*Let me go.*"

Startled by her vehemence, by the sound of tears in her voice, he released her. "Brandi?"

Just like that, she was gone, dashing into the house and leaving the patio door open. Though his body was still tight, his lust had died, banished by the sight of her stricken face. Sebastian frowned, then cursed viciously. The game had been hers, so why was she acting so upset?

It was past time they talked, understood each other.

He needed to know what was going on, and he needed to know tonight.

He stepped out of the Jacuzzi and stripped off his sodden briefs, wringing them out and tossing them over the back of a chair before putting the cover back on the Jacuzzi. He found a towel and wrapped it around his hips. When he went into the cabin, silence greeted him. Brandi's door was shut. He started to knock on it, to demand she talk with him, let him explain, but he decided it might be more prudent to face her with pants on and his hormones in check. This turbulent anger was almost as bad as the lust, and he needed the iron control he used on the job, the alert consciousness of every detail that made him so successful at providing personal protection.

By the time he felt he had some measure of control and had dressed again, it was late. He tapped on Brandi's door. When he didn't get any immediate reply, he silently turned the knob and peeked inside.

Brandi lay curled on her side like a small child, her hands tucked beneath her left cheek, the blankets pulled over her shoulders. She'd left on the bedside lamp.

Darkness. She really didn't like the darkness. He filed away that small bit of information. To the economical man, it was a waste of money to burn a lamp all night long. But this time, his concern for her fear overwhelmed the worry of expense. He didn't like that she had any fears at all. What he disliked most, though, was that, on some level, she seemed to fear *him*.

Closing the door, he decided to put off their talk for the morning. Sleep was the furthest thing from his mind, so he removed his shirt, shoes and socks, then went and settled himself on the small sofa. He used the remote to turn the television on low and found an all-night movie station.

Hours passed, and he was almost asleep, the movie forgotten, when a small, choked scream awoke him. He was on his feet in an instant, his heart pumping adrenaline. But before he could fully react, Brandi's bedroom door flew open. She took one look at him, let out a low pain-filled moan, and came running into his arms.

BEING HELD TIGHT, feeling the solid thumping of his heart, his warm firm flesh, made her feel a little more secure. But the dream had been so horrible, especially since she hadn't suffered through it in so long. She'd prayed the nightmare was gone for good, but it hadn't taken much to revive it. With a sense of despair, she accepted that the horror would never truly be gone—just as she would never truly be the same person again.

She snuggled closer to Sebastian, wanting to crawl inside him, to hide herself away someplace safe. He rocked her gently, murmuring small nonsense words, and it helped so much just having him close. After several moments holding her that way, he tipped her back just a bit and smiled.

"I gather there's no villain in your room? I don't need to go dashing in like the white knight, after all?"

Brandi shook her head, her eyes wide on his handsome face, her mood solemn despite his gentle teasing.

"And no snake came in the window? No spiders under your covers?"

"No. No snakes, no spiders. Just boogeymen."

"So, it was a dream?"

She was so relieved he hadn't said *just* a dream, that she managed a quavering smile, too. But with the smile, she began to feel foolish. It was more than she could bear, constantly playing the immature fool in his presence. She tried to pull away, but his arms tightened. When the dream had awakened her, she hadn't thought about what she was doing, she'd simply gone looking for Sebastian. Now she wished she'd dealt with the dream as she always had—alone.

"Shh. It's all right, Brandi. Don't run away from me again, okay?"

God. After their disastrous Jacuzzi experience, he had to think she was a ninny—either running to him or from him, unable to make up her mind. She dropped her forehead against his chest, fighting against the tears.

His large hand smoothed over her hair, then moved farther down her back, rubbing up and down her spine. There was nothing sexual in the touch, only comfort. "Come here."

Before she knew what he was doing, he'd sat back on the couch and lifted her into his lap. To her surprise, the position didn't alarm her. It felt secure and warm and cozy. Her long flannel gown was pulled tight over her knees and he lifted her an inch, adjusted her gown with an economical touch, then resettled her again, as if she were a child. It was so amazing to her how different he was from the man who only hours before had been the epitome of raw masculine lust.

With her head tucked under his chin, his arms around her and her legs draped over his own, she seemed to absorb his heat. He was so hot. And his skin... She opened her hand the tiniest bit, feeling his smooth texture, his hardness.... And then she caught herself. She had no business exploring him, leading him on again, when she couldn't do anything about it. He'd already proven earlier tonight that he wasn't interested in her silly brand of timid intimacy. And there was no guarantee she'd ever be able to get past the nightmares, the memories.

She started to pull away, but he gently tightened his hold. She realized he planned to keep her close for a while. She was glad, in spite of herself.

After a soft kiss to the top of her head, he said, "You want to tell me about the dream?"

"No."

She felt his chuckle deep in his chest and some of her grim mood lifted, filled by him instead of the reality of the dream. "But I will. If you're sure you want to hear this. I mean, it wasn't a simple dream."

"I didn't think it would be."

She sighed, wondering where to begin, and decided an apology should probably be first. "I suppose, given the ridiculous way I've acted, I owe you a few explanations."

And he said, "Knock, knock? Brandi, are you in there? How many times do I have to say this?"

She heard the amused exasperation in his words and peeked up at him.

"This is *your* vacation, honey. Yes, I'd like to know you better, to understand you, just like I want you to know me better. But I don't want you to feel pressured. You don't *owe* me anything, especially not explanations. But if you feel up to sharing, if you want to talk, I very much want to listen. Understand?"

Pressing her cheek back to his warm chest, she nodded. The feel of his chest hair was crisp and curly and it tickled her nose. Trying to be inconspicuous, she breathed deep of his wonderful, hot male scent, and almost shivered with the pleasure of it. She could gladly spend the rest of the night just sitting here enjoying the touch and smell of him. She felt relaxed enough to doze off; for once, the nightmare had quickly faded from her mind. But despite what he'd said, there were explanations to give.

Sebastian continued to stroke her, adding to her languor. "You haven't acted ridiculously, Brandi. Granted, I haven't understood everything that's happened, but I never thought you were ridiculous. Don't use that word again."

"Yes, sir."

He gave her a chiding squeeze for her smart mouth, then kissed the top of her head, her temple.

Brandi knew he was waiting, that he wouldn't pressure her. Without thought, she twined her fingers in his chest hair and pressed her nose a little closer while she searched her mind for the right words.

"Brandi?"

"When I was eighteen, I was raped."

It felt as though the world stopped. She probably shouldn't have just blurted it out like that, but how else did you tell such a thing? Sebastian didn't breathe, didn't move. Even the solid, comforting beat of his heart seemed to pause. She was used to that reaction, had felt it with her parents and her sister, Shay. Silent shock, disbelief. A mental distancing, because the truth was ugly and real and people didn't want to share that reality. It left them floundering for the right words, made them uncomfortable.

A familiar lump formed in her throat and she started to shake, but suddenly Sebastian had a hand buried in her hair and it seemed he held her even closer without really moving. His head came down so that his cheek pressed into hers and it seemed as if he were surrounding her, protecting her, as if he could give her his strength.

Brandi drew a shuddering breath. "I know you don't want to hear the details...."

"Yes, I do." His voice was hoarse, and when she leaned back to look at him, his expression was stark. One big, hot hand cupped her cheek, his rough thumb smoothing over her cheekbone. "It's bothering you tonight or you wouldn't have had the dream. That *is* what the dream was about, wasn't it?"

With a tiny nod, she whispered, "I used to have the nightmare all the time, whenever I went to sleep. But over the years, it's gotten better. Now, I hardly ever have it. But I guess with what happened today...."

Sebastian drew a long breath. He lowered his head until their brows touched. His dark lashes swept down to hide his eyes and in a rough whisper, he said, "You mean what I did in the Jacuzzi?"

"No! Well, that is, I didn't like what happened tonight, but the dream was brought on because of those men when we were shopping, not because you rejected me."

His head snapped back up. The light of the television reflected on his face, in his eyes. They were wide-open now and boring into her. "Rejected you? Is that what you think happened?"

She should have been embarrassed, but his incredulous look kept her from feeling anything but defensive. "I know you asked me to touch you. And I would have. I wanted to. But when I took so long, fumbling around and acting like a schoolgirl, you changed your mind."

"God, no." He kissed her forehead, her nose, quick kisses of apology. "No, I just... Brandi, I think there's a lot of things I didn't understand, but none of it was your fault. Hell, I'm supposed to be trained to pick up on stuff. But I've been a typical male idiot, ruled by my hormones and little else."

"I don't know what you're talking about."

His grin was self-derisive. "I thought you were playing a game."

Her eyes searched his. "A game?"

After a big sigh that expanded his chest and drew her attention there again, he said, "We've got a lot of talking to do, I think. Would you like some coffee or hot chocolate?"

She considered that, then shook her head. "I like sitting here. I like...seeing you like this." To explain, she smoothed a hand over his firm broad chest, up his hard muscled shoulders, then to his rough jaw, enjoying the rasping feel of his whiskers on her fingertips.

His eyes closed and he gave her a lopsided grin. "You can stay here all night, okay?" So saying, he sat back on the couch and cuddled her close again. After a second, he laughed, but the sound wasn't one of amusement.

"Brandi, I have to tell you what I thought, so we can clear the air. I don't know any tactful or gentle way to put it, so consider this my apology up front, all right?"

She braced herself for a rejection and nodded. After all, what man wanted a woman who'd been through what she had, who'd been permanently affected by the ordeal? It had taken her years, but she'd gotten her life back in order—all except for the intimacy. And she didn't know if she'd ever be the same as other women in that regard.

With his eyes closed, his head resting back against the couch, Sebastian looked utterly relaxed. "I hope I don't embarrass you, but today in the Jacuzzi, if I'd let you touch me, I'd have come."

Brandi swallowed hard, but thankfully Sebastian still didn't look at her. He shrugged his big shoulders and went on, as if he hadn't just said something so incredibly personal and sexually intimate.

"I didn't want to do that. Not unless and until I was inside you, where I've wanted to be almost since I first set eyes on you." He rolled his head toward her and lazily opened his eyes. "What happened tonight wasn't a rejection, it was self-preservation. You were killing me, being so sweet and seductive and so damn sexy. I can't even look at you without getting hard. By now, I've been hard so long it wouldn't take much to set me off."

He waited for her reaction, his gaze warm and patient. Feelings swamped her—excitement, anticipation...pride. Sebastian, the most gorgeous, incredible man she'd ever known, wanted her. And then reality and remorse hit her at once. She wanted to look away, to shield herself, but that would be cowardly. So she faced him and gave a small, regretful shake of her head.

"I'm sorry. I don't think I can.... I want to. I love kissing you and touching you. I haven't done that, not with any man, since the rape. The fear..." She stopped to draw a shuddering breath, to compose herself and finish what she was trying to tell him. He deserved to know everything. "It comes out of nowhere, when I don't expect it. I get these panicky feelings. I try to push them back, but I can't."

A gentle smile tipped up the corners of his mouth. "Except maybe when you're in complete control? Like when you kissed me by the fire?"

"Yes. I wasn't afraid then. You said I could call the shots and I trusted you to stick to the deal. When I told you not to move, you didn't. If you had grabbed me, or even held me like this, I might have panicked."

"It doesn't bother you now that I'm holding you?"

"No. We're not kissing. You don't look the same now as you did then."

"You mean aroused?"

She nodded, feeling shy in spite of all that they'd discussed. "You have this look, like you did in the Jacuzzi, as if you want to devour me."

"A damn good description." He lifted his hand to her cheek again and Brandi noticed that he trembled. She enjoyed the way he kept touching her, so gently, so carefully. And how he'd pressed those soft kisses to her face, not sexual kisses, just...touching. As if he couldn't help himself.

He sat up and cupped her face fully in both palms. "I want you to know, not just for this vacation, not just for the five days, but for as long as you know me, as long as you need to, you'll always call the shots. I couldn't stand it if I made you uneasy. If I do anything, say anything, just tell me. You can be honest with me. But I don't want to have to worry that I'm screwing up and don't know it."

She nodded again, unable to believe what she was hearing. "Does that mean you want to keep on..."

"Kissing you? Touching you? Damn right."

"You're not...disgusted? That I was raped, I mean. Or that I'm still carrying my fears."

"God, no." He hugged her tight. "Brandi, I won't lie and say I don't wish I could find the bastard who hurt you. I'd gladly kill him with my bare hands. But you're not responsible for what he did. And your reservations now seem perfectly normal to me."

"Do you...do you really want to hear about it?"

Still holding her, he said, "I want to know everything about you. What makes you smile, what makes you cry. What makes you happy, what makes you sad. I want to know your dreams and your nightmares, because it's all part of who you are."

She licked her lips, trying to decide where to begin. Borrowing his tactic, she closed her eyes and just said the truth. "There were three men, not one."

"God." His entire body trembled, then tightened around her.

She heard him swallow, felt his deep breaths. But he didn't say anything else, and she had no clue as to how he felt at that moment, how he might actually react to her very ugly truths. She breathed evenly, calming her mind, calming her heart. Then decided, why not? Perhaps learning it all would repulse him, but then at least she'd know, and it would be over with. Somehow, from the beginning, Sebastian had been able to reach inside her to draw out emotions and feelings she hadn't known still existed. If he was going to take those feelings away, it would be easier now than later.

She pasted on a false smile, but she couldn't quite bring herself to look at him. She would hurry through this, get it over with, then accept the consequences.

"My family and I were aboard a cruise ship in the Caribbean—the last vacation I've taken until now. It was supposed to be fun. I was feeling very grown-up—I'd just turned eighteen—almost a woman, so I flirted. With the wrong men. It was exciting, at least until I started to get tired. I left my parents and Shay at a party on the upper deck and went back to our state-room. I didn't know it then, but the men had followed me. And because I thought Shay would be the only one coming in, I hadn't checked the door. One of my shoes was in the way and it hadn't closed tight. The men didn't even have to knock."

It was getting harder and harder, and it had been so long since she'd rehashed the details. Her chest hurt and her throat felt ready to close. She became aware that Sebastian was stroking her again. She felt his strength and, at the moment, she needed it.

Everything was blurred and she realized that in spite of her resolve, tears had welled in her eyes.

"I yelled and yelled, but they'd slipped in while I was asleep, and I didn't wake up until the door was closed tight behind them. No one heard me screaming. And they were already on me. They...they called me names. And they slapped me, because I wouldn't stop crying and screaming."

Sebastian lifted her hand to his mouth and held it there against his parted lips. She could feel his teeth, the quickness of his breath. He remained silent, though, and she waited. Waited for questions, for suspicions. There were none.

"No one knew what had happened till the next day. Shay and I were sharing the cabin, but when she came in, I couldn't quite bring myself to tell her about it. I should have. It was so stupid of me to just lie there. But I felt numb, almost dead. And so ashamed and dirty and embarrassed. It felt easier to pretend it hadn't happened. Shay assumed I was sleeping. And very early the next day, when we stopped in a port, the men got off. I never saw them again."

Sebastian tapped her knuckles against his mouth, his grip on her hand almost bruising. When at last she looked at him, his eyes were closed, his head bent slightly forward. The muscles in his neck and shoulders were taut, straining. His nostrils flared with every breath he took. But he held still, her hand wrapped securely in his. Her body was bathed in his warmth as he cradled her close on his lap.

It wasn't quite as hard talking to him about it as she'd thought it would be, and she realized with a start that having Sebastian holding her had made all the difference. It wasn't like explaining to the authorities, who had bombarded her with questions while they paced around the room. Or the therapist, who sat there in her chair, looking so cold and detached, despite her sympathetic expression, waiting for Brandi to give away an emotional revelation so she could dissect it and find a *cure*. Even her parents and Shay hadn't been able to just listen. Always they came up with unnecessary apologies and guilt. They'd look at each other, their expressions wounded. She'd always ended up feeling guilty for making them so unhappy.

"At first, my parents were kind of shocked, then so angry. Not at me, but they didn't understand why I hadn't told them what happened. They wanted the men really bad. Thinking back on it, I've decided it was the only reaction they could have had. They made demands of the captain, who asked around and found out I'd been flirting with the men. He didn't accuse me, but he told my parents that I had to learn to be more careful, that you couldn't trust anyone anymore. And he was right. I shouldn't have flirted with strangers. And I should have spoken up right away—but at the time, I just...*couldn't*. Besides, we were in international waters, there was nothing anyone could do."

"Brandi."

There was a wealth of tenderness in the way he spoke her name, but his jaw was rigid, his eyes cold and hard. He looked the same as her parents had—distraught, disgusted. She tried to pull her hand free, but he again pressed it to his mouth, leaving the touch of a hot kiss on her wrist.

Feeling as if she might crumple up and fall away, she asked with a touch of sheltering sarcasm, "Are you happy now that you know it all?"

He wiped a lingering tear from her cheek. "I'm glad you told me, yes. But I'm not happy. I'm probably the most miserable bastard alive."

"Because you're stuck on this vacation with me? No one says we have to spend the time together."

"Oh, Brandi." He shook his head at her in a chiding way. "That's not what I meant."

"No?" Her whole body trembling, she pulled her hand free to wrap her arms around her middle. It was an old habit, one she'd broken herself of, but she fell back on it instinctively. In this situation it was ludicrous, given she was sitting on Sebastian's firm lap. Suddenly she felt cold from the inside out. "I made all the wrong choices, one mistake after another. You must think I'm an idiot."

He ran a hand over her hair, then down her back, moving her just a tiny bit closer to his bare chest. His look was tender and direct and filled with emotion. "The truth, remember?"

She said, "Of course," even though she didn't know if she could bear the truth.

His eyes were sad, but he gave her a small, sweet smile. "What I think is, you're the most incredible woman I've ever met."

6

EMBARRASSED BY the ridiculous compliment, Brandi snorted and said, "You must be awfully easy to impress."

He chuckled. "Actually, no. I'm damn hard to get around, and because of my background, I'm too critical of other people. But after all you've been through, you're still sweet and gentle, not bitter. I think that constitutes a small miracle."

"I may not be bitter, but I'll never be a normal woman again, either."

Sebastian pretended to study her face. "You look fine to me." Then he kissed her cheek, letting his lips linger. "You taste even better. And no 'normal' woman ever pushed my buttons the way you do. If you're not normal, I can only be grateful, because I think you're perfect just the way you are."

She couldn't repress her smile of relief, even though she knew his words were nonsense. "You know what I meant."

Sobering, he said, "Yeah, I do. But it's not true, baby. You're a little more reserved, but you have all the same needs, all the same desires as any other woman." Then he grinned. "You just needed the right man to volunteer his body for your inquisitive mind."

A few remnants of tears were still in her eyes and she wiped them away. He gave her that tender smile again that made her want to stay with him forever.

But there was so much still in the way. "Sebastian, I don't know if I'll ever be able to make love. Just the thought of..." Her voice trailed away. It was more than difficult trying to say such things, trying to express her problem.

"Hey, no blushing now." His voice was low, whispered against her cheek. "You can tell me anything, honey. There's no one here but us."

The night was quiet. Without her realizing it, the television had gone blank, leaving only a dull glow coming from the screen and a soft hum in the air. Her position on Sebastian's lap put her as close to him as she could get. All around her was his scent, his warmth, his concern and his tenderness. He wore only his jeans; his long legs were stretched out in front of him, and his large feet were bare. A dark, appealing shadow of whiskers covered his lean cheeks and sharp jaw. His eyes were slumberous, his dark shiny hair tousled.

To Brandi, he felt safe and sexy and somehow a part of her. She swallowed, then decided to take advantage of the moment. Another one like it might never come again, and she did have so many questions, so many things she'd like to talk to him about. Sebastian was available and willing and she trusted him, even more than she trusted herself sometimes.

"The thought of a man getting on top of me makes me ill. I...I break out in a cold sweat."

He rubbed his chin on the crown of her head and replied simply, without inflection. "There are other positions, you know."

"But a man is so much stronger. He could always switch positions. And Shay told me once that a man who's really excited doesn't always know what he's doing."

"What?" He tipped her chin up and his frown was fierce. "That's total bull and a miserable cop-out. Men are always responsible for their actions, especially when they're with a woman. Why would Shay tell you such a damn stupid thing?"

His vehemence startled her, but didn't alarm her. "She'd talked me into going on a date. But the guy got...pushy. He didn't really do anything, just tried to steal a kiss."

"A kiss you didn't want to give him?"

"Yes. But I guess he thought he could convince me."

"I hope you slapped his damn face," Sebastian muttered.

A slight grin twitched at her lips as she shook her head. "I wish I had, but instead, I ran. I get panicked and I can't think about anything except getting away."

"Is that what happened today while you were shopping?"

Amazed at how easy it was to talk to him, even

through her embarrassment, she nodded. "Two men tried to pick me up."

"I wish I'd seen them."

Brandi laughed at his look of mean intent. She liked it that he felt defensive of her, even though she wanted and needed to learn to defend herself. "It wasn't that big a deal. Shay says I make too much of things sometimes, and she's right. She said that just because a man shows his interest, or steals a kiss, doesn't make him a rapist."

"I'd say she's right. But I'd also say anyone, male or female, should know how to accept no as an answer and to respect another person's wishes. Don't let Shay talk you into doing anything you don't want to do."

"She talked me into this vacation."

"Except for this vacation," he clarified quickly, then gave her a lopsided grin. "In this one instance, Shay was brilliant."

Brandi shook her head. "Actually, I shouldn't have been surprised by what she did. She's made it her personal goal to get my life jump-started. She feels... responsible somehow, for not watching out for me on the cruise. I keep telling her it wasn't her fault. It was my fault."

"No. You were eighteen, sweetheart. You didn't ask to be violated, no more than any woman does. Leaving your door unlocked doesn't warrant blame for you or in any way serve as an excuse for what those bastards did. It was just a small mistake that cost you more than it should have."

"But I had been flirting."

"So? Flirting is something everyone does. It's human nature, not an invitation to brutality. The only people at fault were the men who took advantage of a young woman's innocence."

"I've wished so many times that I'd done things differently."

"We all do. But we're human, and we have faults. That's just something we all have to learn to live with."

Brandi couldn't help but relax. Sebastian was so open and honest in his responses. He didn't seem bothered by the topic, didn't seem hesitant in answering her. She gave him a small hug. "Talking with you is so different from talking with my family."

"How so?"

"They don't really want to hear about any of this. It makes them uncomfortable. They don't know what to say, and they're afraid they'll upset me. Usually they end up apologizing. Again and again. We've made a sort of silent pact not to bring it up, to pretend it never happened. They don't know about the nightmares. I didn't want to worry them or add to their ridiculous guilt, and there's nothing they can do about them anyway. The dreams are just something I have to learn to deal with."

Sebastian cursed softly, confusing Brandi, then he looked at her again. "I'm glad you're sharing it with me, then. And I want you to feel free to tell me anything. Ask any question you want, hold on to me when you need to. Everyone needs to talk. About everything. Keeping things inside never helps."

Brandi hesitated for a moment, uncertain how to verbalize what she was feeling, but she wanted Sebastian to know, to understand how much this time with him meant to her. Usually, with her parents or with Shay, she ended up being the one listening. They needed her to understand that they felt guilt, that they suffered, too, over what had happened. But with Sebastian, he listened and accepted. She could pour out her heart, and it felt good. Somehow, the living nightmares—the ones that stayed with her every hour—weren't quite so overwhelming anymore.

There was no way to put all that into words, so finally she just whispered, "Thank you."

He hesitated, then cautiously, with his lips first on her temple, then her cheekbone, he kissed his way toward her mouth. When his lips touched hers, gently, without pressure, she sighed. So close their noses touched, he looked into her eyes and she could see his smile, could feel the warmth of his incredible green eyes.

"You're welcome." His husky whisper made her tingle.

She had to close her eyes to shield some of the heavy emotions she felt before she could make her next confession. "Sebastian, I like kissing you."

"Do you?"

She smoothed her hand over his bare shoulder again and noticed the muscles were more relaxed now. She looked back to his face and shivered at the sensual heat in his eyes; his masculine interest was so plain to see, so natural. He hid nothing from her, and maybe that was what made it less frightening.

"I've been so curious for so long. But I was afraid to chance getting close enough to anyone to do the things most girls have done by the time they were teenagers. I was a late bloomer. I didn't get asked out much, especially not with Shay around. She's so gorgeous, most of the boys my age were too busy staring at her to even notice me."

"I noticed you."

Brandi grinned. "I know. It still amazes me that you aren't involved with Shay."

He snorted. "Your sister terrifies me. There's no denying she's beautiful, but in a different way from you. Shay doesn't have a subtle bone in her body. She's extravagant and pushy and arrogant."

"She's incredible."

He laughed. "Don't get defensive. I like your sister a lot. And her personality suits *her* to perfection. But Shay has a way of making mincemeat out of the males of our species, and I have no desire to do battle with her."

"You make her sound like an Amazon."

"Close."

Brandi smacked his shoulder. "I'm surprised you escaped. She puts most men under her spell within minutes."

"Including all the boys you knew when you were growing up?"

"Mmm. I was just known as Shay's little sister. It didn't give me much of a chance to experiment when most other girls were getting their first kisses—or more. Then after the rape... Well, I wish now that I'd had at least one boyfriend somewhere along the way."

Sebastian was curiously still. "Are you saying, except for the rape, you're a virgin?"

"Yes. But even more than in the physical sense. I...I'd only been kissed a few times, and those were tiny pecks. But I'd dreamed about doing those things, about finding the right guy and..."

She couldn't put her thoughts into words, but Sebastian understood. "You wanted to experience all that first excitement, the first kiss, the first touch. Necking and petting, but being too cautious to go all the way." As he'd spoken, his fingers had slid up and down her arm over the flannel of her nightgown, giving her goose bumps and making her feel some of what he described.

"I like it when you touch me, Sebastian. And I like touching you. You feel so different from me." Her hand stroked his collarbone, his warm throat. His flesh there was taut and silky smooth over hard bone and muscle.

Sebastian wrapped his fingers around hers and kissed her palm. Still holding her hand, he lifted it and moved her knuckles over his chin, his jaw. All the while, he watched her face closely. "Have you ever felt a man's beard?"

The hot look in his eyes made it hard to speak, but she managed a nod. "My father's."

His chuckle was deep and intimate. "This is a little different, isn't it?" He skimmed her hand over his upper lip, where a mustache would be in very few days if he didn't shave. His breath felt warm against her palm.

Without conscious decision, she opened her hand and cupped his cheek. His own hands went to her waist, holding her loosely, leaving her free to do as she pleased, without his interference. In a breathless whisper, she said, "Yes, it's different." *And amazing and intriguing and exciting.* "You're always so warm."

He made a choked sound, then briefly pressed his face into her unruly hair. "I have a beautiful, sexy woman on my lap. It's a wonder I'm not on fire."

She didn't pay any attention to his words. She wasn't beautiful, only passably pretty, but he did make her feel sexy. Enthralled, she felt his jaw move as he spoke, as he swallowed. She watched his throat, trailed her fingertips there, feeling the coarseness of his beard stubble, the thickness of his neck, the steady beat of his pulse. She touched the hair at his nape, then touched it again. It felt cool and deliciously silky. "I never thought of men as having such soft hair."

His eyes watched her, never blinking. "My beard is rough, but not the hair on the rest of my body."

That slowed her, making her stomach tingle. It was a pleasant feeling, like a tickle deep and low inside her.

She looked at his chest hair, dark and thick, covering his broad chest, circling his small brown nipples. She ran her tongue nervously along her lips, then decided to be daring. She reached out. Sebastian closed his eyes for a moment, then opened them again, pinning her. His nostrils flared on a deep breath and she spread both hands over his chest.

Hard and solid. Incredible heat. And a pounding heartbeat.

"Brandi?" His tone was coarse and low. "I like you touching me, sweetheart."

She felt the drift of his warm breath as he spoke, and then she felt the hardness beneath her bottom and knew he had an erection. Curious, she looked up, meeting his gaze. He smiled, reassuring her with that look.

"I'm not going to move, and I won't touch you unless you ask me to. But I'm a simple man who is very attracted to you. I can't help my reactions."

"I don't think there's anything simple about you." She moved her hands to his upper arms, amazed at his bulk, at the way his muscles clenched and pulled without him seeming to move at all. Even using both hands, she couldn't circle his biceps. He still reminded her of a mountain, all imposing, solid strength. And the heated look in his eyes often bordered on savage.

After a while, she really did feel comfortable touching him, and that surprised her. It seemed so natural to be here with him. And Sebastian, true to his word, hadn't moved, other than shifting slightly in his seat and breathing a little harder. She cupped his cheek again, drifted her fingers over the bridge of his nose, his brow. Then she touched his eyelids and watched them flutter shut. He held perfectly still.

"I like how you look at me, with your eyes half closed." Before she said it, she hadn't known it was true. At first, his intensity had frightened her. Then she'd merely been cautious. But now, she supposed she was already getting used to it, the way he seemed to see into her thoughts, the way he looked at her as if no one else mattered. It made her feel special, but not threatened. Not anymore.

"What else do you like?"

She didn't hesitate. "The way you smell."

His eyes opened again. They encouraged her, and she leaned forward until she was very close to him, her nose nearly touching his throat. The scent of him was enough to make her toes curl. She nuzzled his throat, along his shoulder.

He groaned low and deep. When she lifted away from him, he gave her a cocky smile, but his chest moved with his deep breaths. "How do I smell, Brandi?"

She touched the bridge of his nose again and explored a small lump that accounted for the very slight crook there. It had probably been broken at one time. There was a tiny scar at the corner of his mouth and it drew her fingertips next. Everything about him fascinated her.

"It's hard to describe. You smell warm, very warm.

And like musk and spice." As she touched the small scar, his lips parted just the tiniest bit. He licked his lips, and his tongue touched her fingertips. She drew back, shocked at the almost violent sensations that swirled in her belly.

Sebastian stared at her. "Touch me again."

It wasn't a command—closer to a plea. "I..."

"It startled you when you felt my tongue?"

"Yes."

"What did you feel? Inside, I mean." His gaze searched her face, probing, looking for answers. Then his face went carefully blank. "Did I frighten you?"

"No." It wasn't fear that had stolen her breath. But she didn't think she could put it into words. "I've never felt it before, so it's difficult."

"Do you want to continue?"

She nodded, but she wasn't at all certain *where* to continue.

Sebastian settled that problem for her. "How about if I tell you what I felt?"

Her heart raced. The air inside the cabin seemed to be too hot, too thin, even though there was no fire in the fireplace. She felt the tensing of his hard-muscled thighs and squirmed a little, then smiled inside at his reaction. She liked affecting him this way, liked knowing that he wanted her so much.

Keeping his gaze locked to her own, he said, "I felt a rush of heat. Under my skin, inside my muscles. Everything clenched." He grinned. "You're sitting on my lap, so I think you felt it. In my stomach, my thighs.

And here." He pressed the back of her hand low on his abdomen. "There's this sweet pressure. Like anticipation that's hot and thick."

Every single thing he mentioned, she felt. Her own belly was tingling with a delicious ache. "You scare me."

He pulled back, but this time it was she who held on. "I don't mean..." Frustrated, she shook her head and said, "It's not fear that I'll be hurt. It's just that I've never felt this way before. Ever."

He brought her hand to his mouth and pressed a tender kiss to her palm. "What happened to you slowed you down a little. You were still too young to have explored your own sensuality before the rape, and afterward, you were too wary. But now, with me, you feel safe." He smiled at her. "Am I right?"

"Yes." But she had to be honest. "To a certain degree."

Nodding he said, "I think I understand your rules now. Earlier, in the Jacuzzi, I thought you were playing a game of dominance, that you didn't want me to move so you could tease me. And I liked it, believe me I did. But then it was just too much and I couldn't hold back any longer.

"Now I know you weren't playing at all. I understand why it's important for you to be in control." He kissed her again, a quick light kiss that took her by surprise, but thrilled her all the same. "Feel free to satisfy all your curiosity with me. When I first told you that you were in charge, I hadn't exactly had this in mind.

Or maybe I had, but not with any real expectations. Just a lot of hope."

Brandi laughed. Bantering with a man, sexual teasing and innuendo, wasn't something she was used to. But with Sebastian, it felt so natural and right, there was no threat, only fun. She grinned and he grinned with her.

As he tucked an errant curl behind her ear, his smile faded and his look became serious again. "Now that I do understand, I want you to feel free to direct me, to tell me what you want and what you need. You can touch me anywhere you want, however you want. Whenever you want. If you don't want me to move, I won't. If you want me to touch you back, I gladly will. But only if you tell me to. You really are in charge, babe, in every sense of the word."

SEBASTIAN WATCHED as she considered all he'd said. He kept his face carefully masked so she wouldn't know how she'd torn him up inside. At that particular moment, there were any number of people he'd like to light into, not the least of which was her family. Though he had no doubt they'd been misguided by love and their damn guilt, they'd still stifled Brandi's need to talk about the rape, to rid herself of pent-up hurt and anger and fear.

It almost sounded to him as if she'd buried the pain in order to protect them, when it should have been the other way around. But he remembered the guilt he'd suffered for his mother, and knew their lack of understanding hadn't been intentional. Often the victim's loved ones suffered as much—in a different way—as the victim. He'd seen it in his work, as well.

He would have liked to get hold of the men who'd dared to touch her. They'd tried to steal her innocence, her sweetness, but luckily they hadn't succeeded. Despite what Brandi seemed to think of herself, she was simply too strong to lose her will.

But most of all, he felt anger at himself. In his job, he dealt with trauma, both emotional and physical, on a regular basis. He protected women threatened by their abusive husbands, he watched out for the innocent who were stalked for money or political gain. He knew the signs and understood the fears. But he hadn't been himself since first setting eyes on Brandi. He'd let all her signals slip past him, his brain too cluttered with lust and his own vulnerability to see anything else.

He'd actually dealt with rape cases on many occasions. But instead of viewing her caution and curiosity as the residual effects of a trauma, he'd assumed she was playing sex games with him. He'd thought she was using her shyness and need for control as a way to build the sexual tension. Damn his ego.

Now that he knew the truth, though, he had a plan of action. His lust would have to go on hold, but he could deal with that. He *would* deal with it, even if it killed him. Nothing was as important as reassuring Brandi, showing her that she was a woman in every sense of the word.

Her curiosity was starting to bloom, and he'd be

damn sure that he was the man who satisfied it. Any amount of sexual discomfort was worth the final reward. But already, he was literally aching with anticipation.

"You want me to...touch you?"

He grinned at her self-conscious expression and rosy cheeks. Perching on his lap in her virginal gown, her dark hair wild and her blue eyes round, she looked more enticing than ever. Her small bare feet were feminine, her scent sleepy and warm and delicious. Grinning hurt, but it was either grin or groan, and he wanted to reassure her, not scare her with his lust.

"Yes, I want you to." Leaning forward, he kissed her, another light, teasing peck that he hoped would eventually evolve into more. "I want you to feel free to use me. To touch me whenever you want, to kiss me or look at me any way you choose."

"I couldn't."

She said it, but she didn't look sincere. He chuckled. "You already have. And I know if you're this fascinated with my chest, the rest of my body has got to be of interest to you, too."

She gulped, then heaved a big breath. "Are you saying you'd let me..."

"You didn't finish your sentence."

She licked her lips. Her eyes were bright and she had the most adorable expression on her face, a mixture of uncertainty and greed. "I don't know if I could. I mean, I can't predict when the fear will hit me."

The words felt like a blow, erasing all his humor. "I

know. And it doesn't matter. If you change your mind, at any time, there's no pressure. Just say no. That's all."

"You say that now. But if we'd already been... involved, you might feel differently."

"And you're afraid I'd lose control?"

"I don't think you'd deliberately hurt me."

He accepted the fact that it would take time to earn all of her trust, but it wasn't easy. Determined to make as much headway as possible in the five days allotted to him, he decided to throw out the only viable solution he could come up with—even if the very idea of it made him uneasy. "If you ever start to worry about me losing control, you could always tie me to the bed."

She stared at him, her eyes wide with incredulous surprise.

"I'm serious, Brandi. I want you to be comfortable with me, and if that's what it takes, then so be it." Seeing her reaction helped firm his resolve and returned his humor. "Of course, you'd have to promise to be gentle with me, to treat my poor body with respect."

She gave him a playful smack while a grin tugged at her lips.

"And absolutely no tickling. I can't stand it."

"So you're ticklish?"

He sent her a mock frown. "I don't like that wicked gleam in your eye. Promise me right now."

"All right. I promise not to tickle you." Then she whispered, "Not while you're tied down."

He pretended to consider her words, while in truth he was thrilled at the easy way she bantered with him.

And her tone, when she'd spoken, had been husky with promise, with expectation. More progress. At least, he chose to see it that way.

"All right, we're agreed." Then he reached around her for the remote and switched off the television.

With obvious alarm, Brandi stiffened in his arms. "What are you doing?"

"Not what you probably imagine." He tugged on a glossy dark curl that laid over her temple. "Did you think I planned to stand up and strip off my jeans?"

"I don't know." She searched his face. "None of this is like anything I could have ever expected."

"Well, you can relax. I just thought we ought to get some sleep tonight. It's late."

"Oh." She looked down, but he hadn't missed the disappointment in her expression. She started to rise. "I suppose I should get back to my bed."

His arms tightened around her, keeping her gently in place on his lap. "Actually, I thought we might sleep right here. I'm comfortable, and after holding you this long, the thought of my cold lonely bed doesn't appeal one bit."

He could see how badly she wanted to accept, and tenderness the likes of which he'd never felt before threatened to choke him. She looked up, her gaze wary once again. "I'm not too heavy?" she asked.

"Honey, you don't weigh any more than a blanket."

"I might have another nightmare."

Which was one of the reasons he wanted to keep her close. He'd do his best to protect her, even from her own demons. "If you have a bad dream, you can hold on to me. You won't be alone."

Tears welled in her eyes and he couldn't bear it. He tucked her head under his chin, then stretched out his arm to grab a throw on the back of one of the chairs. He spread the cover over them, propped his legs up on the coffee table and leaned back. Brandi shifted a few times, making him painfully aware of his aroused state, but he gritted his teeth and held in his moan of pleasure.

"Sebastian?"

"Hmm?"

"Good night."

Now that felt right. Holding Brandi, listening to her gentle breathing, hearing her tell him good-night. It was something he could get used to, something he wouldn't mind hearing for the rest of his life. He pressed his cheek to the top of her head and felt her wildly curling hair tickle his nose. So soft, so damn sweet. "Good night, babe. Rest easy."

She sighed into him. "I will."

And just as she'd done in the limo, she passed out, going boneless within a minute.

It took Sebastian longer to relax. He tried to remember what he'd been like, how he'd behaved, back when he'd first begun experimenting sexually. It was a very long time ago—a lifetime. He didn't like remembering, because those days had been full of poverty and sadness and desolation. He'd started too young, trying to find comfort with the neighborhood women who needed the distraction as badly as he did.

After he joined the service, he'd gotten more particular, and there were times when he'd gone long stretches without the touch of a woman. Most times he hadn't missed it much, but when he had, he'd easily found feminine comfort. And always, he'd stayed in control—no ties, no commitments.

Now here he was, fully committed to Brandi. Knowing she'd missed her sexual maturity filled him with a primitive greed, both emotionally and physically. She was his. Regardless of the rape, he would be her first man, her first lover.

She sighed in her sleep and he smoothed his hand over her waist, then down her hip to her thigh. It had been an automatic touch, not something calculated, but it thrilled him anyway. She felt so slender, so delicate. The flannel gown was soft and somehow suited her perfectly, though he thought her own skin would have suited her even better.

Images filled his mind and he closed his eyes, relishing them. She would be his, he was determined. He still had four days, and he'd make the most of them before his time was up.

First thing in the morning, he would begin.

He grinned, knowing what he planned was a little underhanded, but Brandi needed control, and he wanted to give it to her. The trick was in making her think she held the reins, when in truth she'd be following his lead.

7

SEBASTIAN CONTINUED to rub the towel over his damp body even though he knew Brandi stood frozen in the bathroom doorway. He'd been at it for fifteen minutes or more, just waiting for her to show up. Under normal circumstances when alone with a woman he wanted—who he knew wanted him, too—he would have been oblivious to his nakedness, most likely because the woman would have been naked as well.

Not so with Brandi standing there, her flannel gown dragging the floor, her eyes still puffy from sleep, her soft lips parted in shock. He could feel her curious gaze burning over his body and he wanted to pull her close, to feel the inquisitive touch of her hands, her eyes...her mouth.

He pretended indifference, but in fact he was wound so tight he hurt.

The weather matched his mood, waking him this morning with a powerful thunderstorm. Rain slashed the windows and the sky appeared as dark as early evening. He'd slipped away from Brandi after a loud crack of thunder and he had purposely left the bathroom door ajar as he'd showered. He'd hoped the sounds of the running water would eventually wake her, even though the storm hadn't. Of course, she'd been snuggled up close to him then, warm and secure. He'd felt the chill of the room as soon as he'd left her, and though he'd tucked the blanket around her, he'd thought that the loss of his warmth might be enough to rouse her.

He wanted her familiar with him and his male routine. He wanted her comfortable with his body. The more she thought of him as just a man, male to her female, the less she'd think of him as a dominant counterpart to her feminine vulnerability. The mundane chores of shaving and bathing and eating would help lower him to the status of just another flesh-and-blood person.

Finished drying, he slung the towel around his shoulders and turned to face her with a wry grin on his lips, but Brandi didn't notice. Her gaze was nowhere near his face. He cleared his throat and she jerked. When her eyes rose quickly to meet his, he asked, "You okay, babe?"

"You're naked."

"Am I? Damn, that's right." He mustered up a puzzled look. "I took my clothes off to shower. That's usually how it's done, you know."

Brandi slowly and carefully licked her lips, her gaze now glued desperately to his. "You're...awfully big."

Chuckling, he deliberately looked down at himself—and saw he was thankfully still inattentive to the fact of a very appealing female in the area. "Hmm.

And I'm not nearly so impressive as I can be." Then he looked at her. "Does it bother you?"

She shook her head, her dark curls moving around her pale face, and her eyes again went over his body. She said softly, "I wasn't talking about that. I meant you were just so massive. All over."

"I know. I was teasing you."

"Oh." She looked around, then shrugged. "The door was open."

"I wanted to hear you if you woke up," he said with a straight face.

Brandi nodded. "The storm woke me."

Damn. He couldn't very well stay unenthusiastic if she continued to watch him this way. He had to distract himself, so he moved to the sink and turned on the hot water, then opened his shaving kit.

"What are doing?"

There was less shocked reserve in her tone, and more natural curiosity, which is what he'd been counting on. He flicked her a glance and saw that she'd stepped a little closer. He treated his nudity as natural, and she seemed to be attempting to do the same.

"I'm going to shave." Then he added casually, "I don't want to scratch you with my whiskers if you decide to do any of that touching or kissing we talked about."

She remained silent, her eyes boring into him, over him. Squirting the shaving cream into his hand, he asked, "Have you ever watched a man shave?"

"No."

"Not even your father?"

"My dad's very private. Besides, he and Mom had their own bathroom."

Flipping down the toilet seat, Sebastian said, "Come on in and sit. I don't mind the company."

"I...um..." He watched as she shifted her feet, her hands clasped together in front of her, then she blurted, "Okay, but could you wait just a moment? I'll be right back."

Before he could answer she darted out. Sebastian chuckled. Of course, she needed a trip to her own bathroom. He only hoped she didn't stop to change clothes. He liked her in the loose-fitting flannel gown with the tiny blue flowers all over it. Its Victorian styling suited her.

He didn't want her to comb her hair or splash her face, either. He liked seeing her all sleepy-eyed and warm and tousled. She looked sexy as hell and so sweet, his stomach muscles ached from being pulled so tight.

She returned a moment later, her hair still wild and disheveled, her gown in place and her blue eyes bright. She rushed forward and took the seat beside him, which put her eyes on a level with his navel. *Damn.* He'd never survive this.

"Go ahead."

He laughed. "Intend to enjoy the show, do you?"

She'd regained enough of her impudence to stretch out her legs, cross her ankles and lean back against the commode. "You offered. It's certainly not something I'll get to see again anytime soon."

"Ah, now there you're wrong. You can watch me shave any time you like. All you have to do is tell me." So saying, he started by spreading the shaving cream around his face, then went through the contortions all men employ to reach those hard-to-shave places. Brandi sat in fascinated silence beside him. Amazingly, her gaze was as much on his face and the process of removing whiskers as it was on any other part of his body.

He was almost done. As he swiped the razor one last time across his jaw, Brandi said softly, "You look so hard."

He nicked himself and cursed, but when he turned to her, he saw her staring at his hip where his skin was a shade lighter from being forever protected from the sun. She lifted her hand slightly from her lap, then lowered it again.

Sebastian grabbed up a facecloth and wiped his jaw before turning to face her fully. He couldn't help himself, his body stirred with her interest, and being that he stood there completely naked, hiding his reaction wasn't an option.

Her gaze flicked to his face, then back to his swelling erection. She looked absurdly amazed, and he tried to grin, tried to muster up one ounce of humor, but failed.

"You...you get excited just because I'm looking at you?"

Rather than answer her, he let his own gaze linger

over her body as she lounged back in feigned negligence. He could detect the soft mounds of her breasts, the slight curve of her belly, the gentle slope of her thighs. He took his time, letting her *feel* where he looked. She shivered and her cheeks flushed—but not with embarrassment.

"You react when I look at you, too, babe. It's just that your body isn't as obvious as mine. But if a man is smart, if he knows where to look, it's plain to see." His tone was low and gravelly and there wasn't a damn thing he could do about it. Without moving closer to her, he reached out his arm and very gently, with only the barest touch, circled a pointed nipple with his forefinger. Brandi gasped and her eyes closed, but she didn't pull away. "This is a small clue."

Her lips parted while she breathed deeply. "I liked that."

She sounded amazed, not at all repulsed. "Good. Should I do it again?"

Her eyes opened and she stared at him. Biting her bottom lip, she gave a tiny, uncertain nod.

To most people this might have seemed to be the most bizarre situation—a woman covered from neck to toe in sturdy flannel, a man buck naked and on display, leaving himself vulnerable, doing no more than touching one sweet soft breast. To Sebastian, though, it meant he'd made incredible progress. He wanted to shout with his success—Brandi wanted him to touch her in a sexual way. Nothing else mattered to him at the moment.

His hand trembled a bit as he reached out again. He wanted to move closer, to touch her everywhere, to give her unbearable pleasure and hear her moaning his name, hear her crying out in an intense, mind-blowing climax. But he was also afraid of doing one little thing wrong and spooking her. He didn't dare push her too far too fast.

He toyed with her nipple, still using only that one fingertip. He brushed against her, used the edge of his nail for a more tantalizing stroke, circled and flicked until Brandi panted and said in a tiny, almost indistinguishable voice, "Please."

He was so hard, he hurt. His erection pulsed with every heartbeat, but Brandi was now oblivious to everything but her own body. Sebastian licked his lips and whispered, "Both breasts, all right, honey? You'll like this, I promise. But if you don't, just say so."

Not giving her a chance to think about it, he lifted his other hand and this time he cupped her breasts, feeling them warm and firm in his palms. Her heartbeat thundered. Brandi made a strangled sound and her gaze remained glued to his face. He knew she was watching for any loss of control, so he did his damnedest to hide the level of his arousal. He couldn't remember ever being so primed, so hot. But Brandi's innocence, her trust, was both a powerful aphrodisiac and a potent reminder of who she was to him. More than he wanted anything, including his own pleasure, he wanted hers. He wanted her to trust him enough to let go, to give herself over to him for safekeeping while the pleasure swamped her and left her insensate.

Luckily, his arms were long, keeping him a safe distance from her. It gave her the room she needed to feel secure. It also afforded him an incredible view of her body; the way her stomach muscles fluttered, the way her thighs tightened, how her throat worked and her hands clenched.

He breathed as deeply as she. "Do you like this, sweetheart?"

"Yes."

That one word sounded like a moan, and Sebastian had to clench his jaw to hold in his own guttural sounds of approval. "Honey...I'd like to try something else, okay? No, don't look at me like that. I'm not planning a wicked perversion on your person. You're the boss, remember? I'm just going to make a suggestion."

It took her a moment, but she finally said, "All right."

His appreciation for flannel doubled as he felt her small breasts swell and fill his palms. He continued to pleasure her breasts as he spoke. "You like my fingers and hands on you here. But I think you'd like my mouth even more."

Frantically, she shook her head, her eyes going wide.

"Shh," he soothed, his fingers still taunting, teasing. "Just listen a minute. You could stand on the toilet lid. I'll even put my hands behind my back if you want. And if I do this and you don't like it, you can just say so. No arguments."

He could tell she was tempted and he held his breath.

"I don't want to take off my gown."

"You don't have to."

"Those men...the ones who raped me." Her voice trembled and Sebastian automatically stilled, his heartbeat frozen. "They told me I wasn't much to look at, that I was all bones and no meat. They...they laughed at me. I know I'm too skinny. Shay is always teasing me about needing a few pounds. My mother says I just take after her, that I won't round out until I have kids. But since I'd never thought to do that—have kids, I mean—I figure I'll always be too small."

Goddamn them. Violent emotion slammed through him, making him want to crush those responsible for stealing away her confidence, her self-esteem. And even her family had added to her insecurity. Couldn't they see how they'd hurt her with their careless remarks? They should realize, with what she'd been through, how sensitive she would be.

Shay would be devastated to hear of her part in this, but he damned well ought to tell her, anyway. He knew she loved Brandi and wanted the best for her. It wasn't in Shay to deliberately hurt anyone, especially not those people she loved.

His eyes burned and his head pounded. He must have looked as violent as he felt, because Brandi scurried off the seat and moved around him, toward the door. He didn't turn to her, didn't try to stop her. No sane words came to his mouth. He wanted to howl in anger and frustration. He needed a minute to get his thoughts in order before he tried to explain a few facts to her.

"Sebastian?"

He shook his head. Without meaning to, his hands fisted and his voice came out in a growl. "They're all idiots. Every damn one of them."

Silence. Sebastian turned and found Brandi still standing there, her expression wary as she seemed to consider his words. "Look at me, Brandi." When her eyes met his, he asked, "Do you think I'd want a woman this damn bad if she wasn't sexy?"

"You don't think I'm too small?"

He did shout then, a low, mean sound that made Brandi jump and take a startled step back. Sebastian was too far gone to heed that small message. He stalked toward her. "You can do anything you like this trip, babe. You can tell me to be quiet, to get lost, to stand on my head if that'll make you happy. But don't you dare believe anything those idiots told you. Listen to me. You're small and delicate and feminine. You're also the sexiest woman I've ever met in my life. And despite my own multitude of sins, I'm not an idiot. I know a beautiful woman when I see one."

Surprisingly, she stopped backing away from him. "You really think I'm beautiful?"

"*Yes!*" He shouted the word, jutting his chin toward her for emphasis, practically looming over her. He watched her flinch, and then just as quickly, she smiled.

With one more perusal of his body, she said, "I think I'll go get dressed now."

He'd forgotten he was naked. Sebastian nodded, though it was the last thing he wanted. "That's probably not a bad idea."

"Maybe you should get dressed, too."

His eyes narrowed at her teasing tone. "What's the matter? You don't want me strutting around the cabin naked?"

She looked to be considering it and he groaned. "Never mind. Forget I asked." He moved past her and down the hall. With every step, he felt her eyes on his backside. Damn, but this was the most stressful trip he'd ever forced himself through.

Then he thought of the look on Brandi's face as he'd touched her breasts, her nipples. It wouldn't be long now. He had to believe that or he'd go crazy. Soon, she'd belong to him. Very soon.

AMAZING HOW A FEW WORDS or a simple occasion could change everything. Brandi left her bedroom feeling much more in charge, sure of herself and her intentions. Now dressed in the long, button-down denim skirt she wore yesterday, slip-on flats and a light cotton shirt, her hair brushed and her face washed, she was ready to face him again.

She was still shy about following through on her new plans; they kept changing on her, expanding, growing more exciting. But she was also anxious to get started.

She found Sebastian standing in front of the living room window, looking out at the storm. He'd pulled on jeans and a white T-shirt, but that was all. His bare feet looked as strong and sturdy as the rest of him. His dark, damp hair had only been finger combed. She liked the look. She liked him.

He'd started a fire and the cabin no longer felt chilly. It seemed perfect to her, to be alone with him this way, on this particular rainy day, closed inside together, safe and warm and isolated from the rest of the world.

Brandi walked up behind him, and when he started to turn, she placed her hand on the solid muscles of his back. "Wait," she said.

He went perfectly still, just as she'd known he would.

The sense of power gave her a forbidden thrill. She smoothed her open palm over the massive expanse of his shoulders. He was such a big man, she marveled.

He was also a gentle, sensual man, and he thought she was beautiful.

"I have a few things I want to say to you, Sebastian, and it's easier if you're not looking at me."

He relaxed, shoving his hands into the back pockets of his jeans. "Shoot. I'm listening."

She drew a deep calming breath, then let it out slowly. "What you did for me this morning in the bathroom? I liked it very much. Thank you."

He turned his head a little toward her, then caught himself and faced the window again. "That was my pleasure. Any time you want to do it again, just say so."

"I intend to, but we'll get to that in a minute." She saw his shoulders tighten, heard him make a rough sound of surprise. She smiled to herself. "I feel a little silly, so bear with me, okay? And don't interrupt," she added when he started to do just that. Brandi knew he'd intended to chastise her for feeling silly, but she couldn't help how she felt, and she wanted him to know. For some reason, sharing her thoughts and feelings with him had become important to her.

"I've been thinking about all this a lot. And since you've convinced me you really do want me, I've decided to make the most of this vacation package. It's never been so easy for me to talk to anyone. But with you, it's like I'm finally free again."

"I'm glad."

She heard the tenderness in his tone, and wrapped her arms around him from behind, pressing her cheek into his shoulder blade. She barely reached his shoulders, even when he was barefoot. But his size no longer intimidated her as it had earlier. Now it intrigued her. He was big and hard and he wanted her.

Pressing a kiss to his flesh, she tried to absorb all the ways he appealed to her. He felt so warm and smelled so good. She loved his scent. Without thought, she opened her mouth and lightly bit him. He sucked in his breath, but didn't move. "Will you take your shirt off for me?"

He did, stripping it quickly over his shoulders and

tossing it onto the floor. He made no move to turn toward her, but every muscle in his body was now clearly defined.

"Since it's raining, we can't really go out today. And I don't want to anyway. I'd much rather stay here and get acquainted with your incredible body and the wonderful way you make me feel."

"Do you realize you're killing me, honey?"

She chuckled, feeling her cheeks warm and her confidence soar. "I know that means you're aroused. And I'm glad." She began touching him again, loving the hot silk of his taut skin, the firm muscles of his shoulders and lower back. "I'd like to do everything, Sebastian, but I don't think I can. At least not yet. But what you said about...about the bed..."

There was a moment of silence, then he swallowed hard and said, "You want to tie me down?"

His voice was almost breathless, holding a mixture of dread and anticipation. Brandi slid her hand around to his hard abdomen and heard him let out a soft hiss. His stomach muscles were ridged, lightly covered by crisp curls that led from his navel down.

"Yes," she whispered, "I'd like to do that. But in a little bit. Right now, I like this. I like touching you without you looking at me. I can see every inch of you, but I'm not embarrassed, not with you turned away.

"I can't be with you in the dark," she continued. "It frightens me. I don't mind admitting that now. When the men raped me, it was so very dark. It took a long time for my eyes to adjust to the darkness, but the panic made it even more difficult. They seemed to be everywhere, and I couldn't tell where I'd be grabbed or groped next. I didn't know what part of my body to try to protect."

"Babe, don't."

It was the only time he'd ever asked her to stop, and she knew it wasn't the words he wanted to end, because Sebastian let her talk. Somehow he knew that talking about it made it easier for her. She wondered now if someone had been attentive, had listened as closely as he did, if she might have gotten on with her life sooner.

But it wasn't the talk, it was the touch that Sebastian protested. Brandi had dipped her hand down until she felt the long solid swell of his erection under his fly. As she spoke, she stroked him, her fingers dragging up and down the rigid length of him. Sebastian was obviously uncomfortable with the mix.

"This is my time, remember? I want to touch while I talk because feeling you, knowing your body, makes the rest seem unreal and unimportant. That's strange, I know, but I'd always associated this with pain and fear. But with you, touching and knowing your body is just...exhilarating."

He tipped his head back on his shoulders and made an attempt to relax. Brandi stepped closer until her thighs were pressed to the back of his. His legs were so much longer, so much stronger than her own, and for now, she thrilled in the differences. His hands were still in his pockets and she said, "Put your hands up behind your head. I want to touch you everywhere."

He groaned, but did as she asked, slowly, like a man being sent to the gallows. Brandi gave him time to get positioned, then she looked him over.

"You're such a beautiful man, Sebastian. So big and hard and powerful."

As she stroked him, her palms finding his taut buttocks, the steel of his upper thighs, his throbbing arousal, she said, "Do you know what I'd really like?"

"Tell me."

"I'd like to give you pleasure."

His knees locked. "You are, babe. You are."

"No, I mean, *complete* pleasure." This was even more embarrassing than she'd imagined, because now she'd have to face him. But first... She unbuttoned the top of his fly.

"Brandi..."

Her name sounded like a warning, but she ignored it. The sound of his zipper rasping down joined the rasp of his harsh breathing. "Tell me if I hurt you."

Another rough groan was her only answer. She felt the power of him through his briefs, then slipped her hand inside the elastic waistband and touched him. Startled, she whispered, "You feel like hot velvet. But alive, and so hard."

The entire line of his tall body went taut. His hands knotted together at his neck, his elbows pulled forward as if straining against imaginary bonds.

Brandi closed her eyes and enjoyed the feel of him.

Her fingers curled around his swollen length, sliding and exploring. Her arms were stretched around him, her body flush against the back of his. Her fingers found the tip of his erection and discovered a spot of moisture. It surprised her, and at the same time gave her stomach an instinctive little curl of pleasure. "Sebastian?"

"Brandi, I can't take much more."

In the face of his need, her embarrassment evaporated. Not looking at him had made this easier, but now she wanted to see his eyes, to judge his reactions, to see him wanting her.

Moving in front of him, she kept her gaze lowered to where her hands touched him, working up the nerve to meet his gaze. Sebastian immediately dipped his head and pressed his cheek to hers, but his arms remained behind his neck. "I want to touch you too, Brandi. Please."

"I...I'd like that. I really would." She buried her face against his broad, comforting chest.

"You said you wanted to give me pleasure. That would surely do it. I'd die to touch you right now."

She whispered, "I'm very afraid of disappointing you and myself."

"I won't let that happen, I swear. Trust me."

She did trust him, but trust had nothing to do with it. Right now it was safe because she knew he'd respect her wishes. But if they removed all boundaries, what might happen? The fact of her body and her fears was all encompassing, taking over other considerations regardless of how she wished it to be.

Slowly, not startling her at all, Sebastian lowered his arms until his hands clasped her wrists. He pulled her hands away from her fascinated study of his erection and put them on his waist. "Okay?"

Brandi nodded. She did feel okay. A little off balance, but okay.

"I'm going to kiss you now."

Brandi knew it wouldn't be a shy or gentle kiss; that's why he'd warned her. But at the moment, she didn't want shy or gentle. She wanted all his greed, all his desire. She only hoped she could accept what he gave. She drew herself up straight and determination filled her.

Turning up her face, she looked into his beautiful green eyes and said, "I'm going to kiss you back."

Sebastian grinned, but as he very slowly lowered his head to hers, the grin faded. He covered her mouth with his own and Brandi didn't have room in her swirling mix of emotions for fear. His mouth was hot and damp and it ate at hers, pulling in her tongue to gently suck on it, then giving her his, stroking over her teeth, teasing and enticing. He nipped her bottom lip and then slanted his head for better access and made love to her mouth.

Through it all, he held back, careful not to loom over her, making certain not to threaten her in any way. His mouth was devouring, but his hands were gentle, merely holding her, not pulling her closer, making no demands.

When she leaned fully into him, her arms around his neck, her body subtly urging against his, he pulled far enough away to say, "Come to the kitchen with me."

A nervous giggle escaped her. "Don't you mean the bedroom?"

"No. The bedroom seems too blatant to start, though we'll eventually get there. I want to make love to you so damn bad. But I'd rather start safe. This means too much to me to screw it up."

"And the kitchen is safe?"

He nodded. "Will you come with me? Will you trust me?"

She really had no choice. Her body pulsed with wanting him and the thought of stopping now made her ache with dissatisfaction. The fear was still there, but it wasn't as strong as the wanting. "All right."

Sebastian took her hand and led the way. Once in the room, he went to the small round kitchen table and pulled out a chair. Brandi started to sit, but he stopped her. "The chair is for me." He caught her around the waist and lifted her to the edge of the table, facing his chair. "I want you here."

Brandi blushed. When he took his chair, the position put him below her, which she felt certain had been his intent. But it also put him between her legs with her long skirt stretched tight between them. His hands rested on the tops of her thighs and his eyes were even with her breasts. He took advantage of the view, his gaze seemingly glued to that particular spot.

"Is this okay?"

Painfully aware that she'd not put on a bra, Brandi nodded. Already she could feel her breasts tightening, her nipples growing stiff, pushing against the fabric of her blouse.

Sebastian muttered something low, then licked his dry lips. "If you don't like this, tell me."

That was all the warning she got before he leaned forward and his hot mouth closed around the tip of one breast, completely enveloping her swollen nipple.

Her breath came in with a whoosh, but with Sebastian situated so much lower than she and his hands idle on her thighs, she didn't in any way feel overpowered by him. She did feel protectively surrounded by him, though.

Twining her fingers in the silkiness of his dark hair, she closed her eyes and relished the feel of his tugging mouth. Even through her cotton shirt, the stroke of his tongue was exquisite torture.

He switched breasts, tantalizing the other nipple while lifting a hand to the abandoned breast. His fingertips found the damp material of her shirt, smoothing it over and around the nipple, as if to soothe it. The dual assault was more than she could take, and she instinctively started to lie back.

Sebastian's other hand supported her spine, keeping her upright. Brandi whimpered.

"Easy, sweetheart."

His voice was a deep rumble, barely heard through the sound of her own heartbeat thundering in her ears. He nipped the tip of her breast, much like he'd done to her mouth, and Brandi felt the small sting all the way to her womb. Her fingers tightened in his hair. "Sebastian..."

She had no idea what she wanted, only that she needed something. He stood, but kept space between them.

"Let's unbutton this skirt a little, okay, sweetheart?"

The possibility of just such a scenario had entered her mind when she'd chosen the skirt. It hung almost to her ankles, but her legs were bare beneath. She'd pulled it on, thinking how convenient it would be to adjust to his greedy hands, and now the fantasy would be a reality. Brandi slipped her feet out of her flats and nodded.

Sebastian had a way of doing things that made them seem so natural and right. He didn't leer at her, didn't start caressing her. He merely unbuttoned the bottom button, down by the hem, then gave her a moment to change her mind.

She remained quiet, waiting, and after a second, he slipped another button free. All his attention was on his hands and her skirt, so Brandi could watch him freely, without him detecting her bright blush or the anxious fluttering of her pulse.

So this was wanting, and in wanting, she hurt with her need for him. She'd never guessed that it would be so strong, so overpowering. She had to bite her lips to keep from whimpering again, this time in impatience.

It seemed to take a long, torturous time before the skirt hung open above her knees. Sebastian lifted the material to the side and stood there surveying her thighs, parted around his hips and hanging over the edge of the table. Still looking at her uncovered legs, he reseated himself, and now her thighs opened even wider to bridge his upper body, fitting beneath his arms. Brandi knew he could see her plain cotton panties in the open V of her legs. Just once, his fingers contracted on her soft thighs, then relaxed.

But when he looked at her, there was nothing relaxed in his expression. His eyes blazed with heat and desire. "I want to make certain you're enjoying this, Brandi."

"I am." She swallowed, then because she couldn't stand a minute more of this, she said, "Make love to me, Sebastian."

His expression tightened, but he shook his head. "Not yet." He was silent a moment before he asked, "Do you know how to measure your own desire, Brandi? Do you know what happens to your body when you're turned on?"

His gaze was intent, and she stared back dumbly, then shook her head. "I only know I want you. Now."

"But it might not be enough." His hands coasted over her thighs, then stilled. She closed her eyes with a sigh, but opened them again when he said, "Honey, look at me."

His cheeks were flushed darkly and his eyes were heavy lidded. He looked so sexy and compelling, she reached for him. "Sebastian."

His curse was low and strained, and he avoided her kiss. "I don't want to hurt you, babe."

"You won't. Sebastian, please."

"Brandi...I have to make sure you're with me before we go any further." His gaze held hers, fierce and intent, while one hand slid further up her thigh. Brandi gasped.

"Is it easier with me looking at you, or would you rather close your eyes?"

She couldn't help but give a strained smile. "Why don't you close your eyes?"

"Because I want to see you." There was a heavy throb of desire in his tone, ridding her of any humor. She could only see Sebastian, only feel Sebastian. His fingers inched closer and closer up the inside of her leg.

Brandi held his stare, unable to look away. And then his nostrils flared and his palm cupped her and he said softly, "Ah." Sensual satisfaction spread over his features, darkening his eyes, sharpening the line of his jaw. "You are ready for me, aren't you?"

The low growl of his voice sank into her, just as his fingers probed, sliding over her soft panties now dampened with her excitement. The realization that she was wet—and he was touching her—caused her to tighten her thighs. But Sebastian was there, his hard body unyielding.

He stared into her eyes, watching her every movement, her every expression. "Don't shy away from me now, babe. Stay with me."

"I don't think..."

"You don't have to think. Just feel." His fingers worked under the edge of her panties, and slowly, so slowly she panted, one finger parted her and pushed deep.

Brandi cried out. Without her permission, her eyes closed and her head tipped back. She would have gladly sprawled on the table except that once again, Sebastian caught her and kept her upright.

"You feel so good, babe. So hot and wet, just the way I want you." His finger teased, pushing in and then out again. Brandi clutched at him, only marginally aware that he now stood before her, holding her close and kissing her face, her ears, her throat. He loomed over her, and there was a moment's alarm, but then he stepped back the tiniest bit and at the same time pressed a second finger deep.

Her body seemed to be suffering some great tension, growing tighter and tighter. It unnerved her, but she didn't want it to stop. With an arm behind her, Sebastian arched her body. He bent and again took a nipple into the heat of his mouth. Brandi cried. She felt the tears on her cheeks, tasted them at the corners of her mouth. Her hips moved rhythmically against his hand, and even though it embarrassed her, she couldn't stop herself from doing it. She didn't feel like herself, didn't feel in any way familiar.

Sebastian encouraged her, slipping his fingers a bit

higher and finding a spot with his rough thumb that made her choke on a scream of pleasure.

"Yes, right there, babe. A little more, okay? Just a little more, Brandi."

She clutched him, her eyes squeezed shut tight, her thighs practically wrapped around him.

"A little more..."

Brandi groaned as a wave of intense pleasure broke over her. Sebastian groaned with her, his arm tight as he murmured and reassured and continued the magic touches. "Yeah, honey, that's right. Come for me. You're mine now, Brandi. All mine."

She heard the soft words, but they didn't make sense. And they didn't alarm her. Not while her world exploded, not while Sebastian held her so close she felt a part of him. And even afterward, when her heartbeat started to slow and her mind reassembled itself, she didn't have a chance to think about the claim of possession he'd made.

Sebastian swept all coherent thought aside by leaning back to smile gently at her, and then asking, "Would you like to tie me down now?"

8

THE GROWING ACHE in his arms couldn't be ignored much longer, but he truly hated to disturb her. Brandi slept soundly, sprawled out over his bare chest, one leg over his hips, her breath fanning his right nipple.

It was a wonder he'd survived.

He grinned, thinking of how enthusiastically she'd participated once she'd had him secured to the bed. All inhibitions had left her and she'd gone about torturing him thoroughly with her curiosity of his body and how it worked.

She now knew firsthand what made him tick, because she'd had him ticking for hours. He had no secrets from her, and that suited him just fine. Even the touchy subject of the condom—and how to put it on him—hadn't slowed her for long. He'd given instructions, and she'd followed them.

She'd made love to him with the most novel approach, unlike anything he'd ever experienced. Because not only did she discover his body, but her own as well. And he'd been able to watch every small nuance cross her beautiful features. Wonder and excitement had been there as often as shyness and reserve.

But as much as he'd enjoyed himself, he really

wished she'd remembered to untie him before falling asleep. Once again, she'd merely passed out, and this time her sleep was undisturbed by bad dreams. Sebastian had even managed to doze for a few minutes here and there. But now he was beyond stiff, starving for food, and getting a little cold since the fire had died down and the rain had stopped, leaving an ominous chill in the air.

He lifted his head to look down at Brandi's body. In the late afternoon light coming through the window, she looked gorgeous. She still wore her shirt, but the skirt and panties were gone. She had a beautiful backside, perfect in shape and texture. The sight of that cute bottom had come close to sending him over the edge several times. He'd wanted to touch her, to squeeze that soft resilient flesh, but by his own suggestion, he'd been helpless to move. It wasn't an experience he wanted to repeat with any other woman. But for Brandi, he'd do it again in a heartbeat. *After* he'd eaten and gotten the circulation back in his arms.

He was just about to say her name, hoping to wake her gently, to soothe her through her unavoidable embarrassment, when a loud knock sounded on the front door. Alarm raced through him. "Brandi? Come on, babe, wake up."

She stirred sleepily. "Hmm?"

Sebastian nudged her with his hips, trying to rouse her. "Damn it, Brandi! Wake up. Someone's at the door."

She lifted her head. "Someone's here?"

She looked totally befuddled and still half-asleep. "Untie me, Brandi."

Rather than doing as he suggested, she sat up, then slipped her slim legs over the side of the bed. She looked around, located her skirt, and started to pull it on.

"Brandi?" His heart thudded heavily as she fastened her skirt. "Untie me."

"Just a minute. Let me see who's at the door first."

"No!" But even as he said it, she started out of the bedroom. *"Brandi!"*

She stuck her head back in long enough to say, "Shh," then was gone again.

Sebastian heard the door open, could hear soft voices, but he couldn't make out what they said. After what felt like an eternity, Brandi returned. She carried a small slip of paper in her hand and she deliberately avoided his eyes.

"It was the front desk. Shay's been trying to get in touch with me. I gather from what the clerk said, she's driving them nuts and she's not happy that we don't have a phone."

He tugged at his bonds. "I don't want a damn phone."

"Me either. But I suppose I should call her back. Otherwise she's liable to land on our doorstep, just to make certain everything's okay. You know how Shay is."

He lifted his head as far as he could to glare at her. "Don't even think about going to the office without untying me first."

"Oh." She blushed, just as he knew she would. "I wouldn't have done that." Then her gaze made note of his exposed body, and she didn't say anything else, didn't make a move to untie him.

"Brandi?"

"Hmm?"

"I loved every second we spent in this bed, but my arms are starting to get a little stiff now."

"Oh!" She rushed up to the headboard and sat next to his chest. The mattress dipped and he rolled slightly toward her, his body bumping her hip. He inhaled her clean, womanly scent—now mixed with his scent and the scent of sex. The ways this woman affected him! He liked it, but it also scared him half to death.

She'd opened to him more today than any woman he'd ever known. At the same time, she'd needed his inability to move, to react to her, in order for her to feel so free. Protective instincts mixed with raw lust could do any man in, but Sebastian was sensitive to women's issues—and to this one small woman in particular.

She finally freed his right hand and he lowered his arm to let it rest lightly over her thigh and around her waist. She leaned over him, her small, perfect breasts only inches from his nose while she tackled the other knot. He'd pulled fiercely against those bindings earlier, needing the pain to counteract his need to hold her. Brandi had been over him, on him, her face taut with pleasure as she worked awkwardly toward her release, and he hadn't been able to help her, to touch her. Watching her helplessly had been its own form of devilish foreplay. He'd shouted with his own pleasure, but Brandi had been too wrapped up in reaching her peak to do more than gasp.

Thinking about it was getting him aroused again. Luckily she hadn't noticed, because that might have ruined all the headway he'd made. *How* he could get aroused again was beyond him. He'd always been a very sexual man with strong appetites, but he'd never been insatiable. Of course, he'd never known anyone like Brandi.

The knots were probably much tighter now than they'd been when Brandi had tied them, thanks to his struggles.

"I've almost got it."

Sebastian smiled. He could hear the concern in her tone, concern for him. He liked that, too. When the knot was undone, Brandi sat back to smile at him. Sebastian stared at her, not moving one iota, then whispered, "Come here."

Without even thinking about it, she leaned down and kissed him. Sebastian knew she didn't note the significance of the kiss, but he did. They were in a bed, he was free to move, and still she'd come to him.

He'd never played sex games before, but damned if he didn't like it with Brandi.

Still not moving his arms, he opened his mouth, inviting her inside, but she leaned back with a grin. "Oh, no you don't. I didn't untie you only to tie you up again. I have to go the registration desk and see what Shay wants." She smoothed her hand over his chest, her expression soft and warm. "Do you want to come with me?"

He slowly flexed his arms, then bit back a groan. "Yeah, I want to go. Can you wait for me to take a shower?"

"Sure. I have to tidy myself up anyway."

He'd hoped she would offer to shower with him, but she was back to looking shy again. Sitting up beside her, he shifted his shoulders, deliberately crowding against her, seeing how much leeway she'd give him now that they were lovers.

Evidently not much. Brandi shot to her feet, her hands twisting in her skirt. She started moving toward the door, her grin slipping just a bit. Sebastian caught her hand. "Why don't you change, and we'll try to find someplace nice for dinner. Maybe even a little dancing."

Brandi blinked at him, her nervousness forgotten, just as he'd wanted. "Dinner and dancing? Are you offering to take me to a nightclub?"

"Sure, why not?" He felt a little ill saying it, the thought of the expense and the waste and the time with strangers not really to his liking. But he wanted Brandi happy, and he didn't want her dwelling on what they'd done all day. Not until bedtime rolled around again—when he hoped very much to sleep with her. Not just to have sex, but to sleep, holding her in his arms all night in a comfortable bed, waking with her snuggled close beside him.

Earlier, he'd told her she was his now. She hadn't acknowledged those words, either to deny or accept them. It had been a tactical error on his part, pushing her too fast toward an emotional intimacy she didn't yet feel. But luckily, she hadn't seemed to hear his declaration, which had bordered on possessive.

She looked confused now. "Do you like to dance?"

He shrugged. "I think I'd like dancing with you."

Of her own volition, she stepped up close to him and hugged his naked body tight. Startled, it took Sebastian a moment to carefully return her embrace. With his mouth touching the top of her head, he asked, "Is that a yes or a no?"

"I don't know how to dance."

That damn tenderness hit him again, almost suffocating, and he closed his eyes. Of course she hadn't done much dancing. She'd been a wallflower, overshadowed by Shay as a teen, then withdrawn from men completely since the rape. There were likely many things she'd never done, and suddenly, he wanted to do them all with her. The cost be damned, because the waste of the money didn't seem like a waste if it made her happy.

"Then we'll definitely go. Trust me, you'll be a natural." He kissed her crown, inhaling her scent and feeling her hair tickle his nose. He loved her hair—the soft, wild curls, the rich dark color. He framed her face with his hands, letting his fingers tangle in those curls, then turned her face up to his. He kissed her gently, trying to ignore the lingering wariness in her eyes.

"We'll do up the town tonight, so wear something sexy."

Laughter replaced the wariness in her beautiful blue eyes. "I don't own anything sexy and you know it."

"Then we'll have to buy you something." Of all the gifts she'd bought, she hadn't purchased anything for herself. She'd only been thinking of the children at the shelter, and he liked that awareness in her. With all she'd been through in her life, she still had room to feel concern for others. She was such a giving, caring woman, it would be all too easy to fall in love with her.

But that thought didn't distress him. He felt good, very good. He'd pick her out a dress more beautiful than anything she'd ever had.

"Sebastian, I don't think..."

He interrupted her, unwilling to listen to arguments. He hadn't felt this enthusiastic about spending money since... Never.

"We've got a lot to do, once you've called Shay. Shopping first, then food, then dancing." He turned her before she could offer more protests, then gave her a light swat on the bottom. "Get going, woman. I'm starved."

SEBASTIAN STOOD BY impatiently while Brandi went through another round of assurances with Shay. She'd been on the phone five minutes now, and from what he could tell from her side of the conversation, Shay wanted a blow-by-blow report of what had gone on, needing to know if she'd made a mistake by rushing Brandi off with a man.

That nettled him. Damn it, he wasn't just any man. Shay knew he had a special sensitivity for women, and she trusted him with many of the situations at the safe houses. So why was she putting Brandi through the fifth degree?

"I promise, Shay, I'm having fun. Honest." Brandi's eyes slanted toward Sebastian, filled with apology and a tinge of embarrassment. "No, it's…it's not like that. He's been…well…"

Sebastian couldn't stop himself. He reached out and plucked the phone from Brandi's hand. She tried to snatch it back, but he held it out of her reach—an easy thing to do given her small stature.

As he put the phone to his ear, drowning out Brandi's muttered complaints, he heard Shay say, "Just remember that he is a man, honey, more man than most. And whether you know it or not, you're a very pretty woman. Don't expect him to keep his distance for the whole trip."

Sebastian rolled his eyes, feeling both annoyance and chagrin. "I'd say she was beautiful, not just pretty, and damn sexy as well. She can handle any man on her own—even me."

A moment of silence, then: "Sebastian."

"Shay," he replied sweetly.

"I, uh…"

"Warning your sister away from me? And after you

donated me to her so nicely. A birthday present, wasn't it?"

"Yes. You were…for her birthday." Then she said in a rush, "I just wanted to make sure I hadn't made a mistake."

He softened, hearing the fretful tone of Shay's voice. He knew she meant well, despite her meddling. Taking charge and running things was simply a part of her. She wouldn't know how to be any other way. "There's no mistake. You trust me, remember."

"Yeah, I trust you. It's just…"

"We've covered it, Shay. Things are fine, and we're having a good time. Both of us." He looked at Brandi and saw her face had gone red. She looked ready to kill him.

He grinned. "I gotta go, Shay. Brandi is anxious to get on with our date." She swung at him, but he ducked and she missed. Chuckling, he said, "If Brandi needs anything, she'll call you. Bye."

"Don't hang—" the receiver hit the cradle and Brandi frowned "—up."

"You don't need her filling you with nonsense." *Or warning you away from me.* "And you don't need her advice. I think we're doing just fine on our own."

She glared at him, but after a moment of him grinning back, her frown smoothed out and she threw her hands up in the air. "All right, I give up. I can't really stay mad anyway, not when I'm secretly glad to be off the phone. But don't ever do that again."

Her frown was back to being fierce, so he quickly

apologized. "I was an arrogant jerk. It won't happen again."

She shook her head, then smiled. "I wouldn't go quite that far. Arrogant, but not a jerk. But you were too high-handed."

"You looked embarrassed."

"Um, Shay being insistent is sometimes hard to talk around."

"Next time, just tell her to butt out." He touched her cheek. "Especially when she's questioning your love life."

Brandi laughed. "Are you kidding? With Shay, that would be as good as admitting there was something going on, and she'd have kept me on the phone forever prying for details. Mostly because I've never *had* a love life."

Sebastian took her arm and steered her toward the exit. Very quietly, he asked, "Is there something going on?"

"You know what I mean."

Of course he did, but he needed to know her thoughts. It had occurred to him that while he grew more and more emotionally involved with Brandi she might very well only be using a prime situation to experiment with her sexuality. He'd invited her to do so. And at the time, it had seemed to be enough.

Now he wanted more.

He'd offered her the use of his body, but he didn't want to be used. Not anymore. He wanted to share. He wanted her trust. Maybe he wanted forever.

Brandi had never experienced lust before, so she had no way of knowing how unique the chemistry was between them. Lust existed, more powerful than anything he'd ever imagined, but it was tempered by so many other, more tender emotions. He wanted to teach her to enjoy her body, to enjoy his body, but he didn't want her to take that knowledge and apply it with another man. The mere thought made him furious.

"Sebastian? Is something wrong?"

"No." He shook his head. "Nothing's wrong."

"You look upset."

He glanced down at her as they walked through the doorway and into the dim, damp outdoors. Sebastian breathed deep, filling his lungs with the rain-scented air, bracing himself. "I'd like for you to sleep with me tonight. The whole night."

Brandi faltered. "I don't know..."

He turned to her, catching both her hands, looking down into her wide blue eyes. "Just sleep, baby. I want to hold you all night, and wake up with you beside me in the morning. Trust me."

The look she gave him now was timid, skittering away before he could figure out what it meant. "I want to trust you, but it's not easy. I really don't think I'd be able to sleep."

"Can we at least try?"

"Why?"

She seemed frustrated, and maybe he was pushing her. But he only had a few days left, including the day they'd have to pack and fly home. Once they returned to the real world, with all the outside commitments of family and jobs and life in general, would she give him a chance? Or would she chalk up her experiences here and try to get on with her life? Was it even fair of him to want or expect more? She'd had so little fun and missed out on so much sensual growth, without a single male-female relationship. But he wanted to be the man to give her those things she'd missed; all the flirting and small gifts and new touches.

He could do it. His lifestyle wasn't so inhibited that he couldn't bend a little and buy her flowers and chocolates on occasion. The thought of squandering the money in such a frivolous way had always seemed repugnant, but to make her happy, he'd do it. He would enjoy doing it.

And his house, though set out in the country away from the congestion of rushing people, was adequate in size, even without all the renovations finished. It wasn't fancy, but it was solid and secure. *A good investment.*

He shied away from that thought, that logical reasoning, because it made him feel like an ass. Brandi needed and wanted fun and laughter, not sensibility. And he'd find a way to give it to her.

The sun peeked out, reflecting on all the wet surfaces, chasing away the last of the clouds. Sebastian leaned down and pressed a quick hard kiss to Brandi's mouth, determined despite her resistance.

"I want to sleep with you because you're warm and soft and smell sweet." Her face flamed and she looked away. Sebastian chuckled. "Besides, I think you'll like it. I know I will. It's a nice feeling to be cuddled close all night with someone you care about."

She didn't deny that she cared, though she did chew on her bottom lip in a fretful way. He counted that as a step forward; what the hell? He was an optimist, and if he chose to count almost everything as progress, it was nobody's business but his own.

"If you don't like it, if it bothers you, we'll deal with it, okay? You liked sleeping with me on the couch."

She stopped, looking down at her feet. "The couch is not a bed, and you were sitting. I know it's silly, but it makes a difference."

"Look at it this way. Last week, did you think you'd find yourself sleeping with a man on a couch, regardless of what position he was in?"

"Last week I couldn't have imagined doing any of the things we've done."

"But you don't regret them?"

She shook her head, and her small smile showed her new confidence. Even more than the belated sunshine, it warmed him. He slipped his arm around her and held her close to his side. "We'll just see how it goes. You can even sleep in that long granny gown if it'll make you feel better."

She blinked at him. "Well, of course I'll wear my nightgown!"

Sebastian laughed at her vehemence. She probably didn't realize how damn sexy the gown looked on her slight frame. Sexy and feminine. It draped her body, hinting at curves, and her rosy nipples showed through the material. Just thinking of it made him semierect once again. He had the hair-trigger reaction of a teenager around her.

And unlike Brandi, he slept in the nude.

He looked at the bright sun. There were way too many hours between now and bedtime. And at the moment, he wasn't at all sure he'd last that long.

THE DRESS HAD COST a small fortune, and Brandi had been very resistant to his buying it. But Sebastian had been insistent and he'd made it a birthday present, so she couldn't really refuse. Now, as he moved her around the dance floor, she knew it was the perfect dress for her. When Sebastian had first seen her in it, he'd given his approval with a low whistle and a heated look that spoke volumes.

She felt sexy, but the sexiness came from the simplicity of the dress—and Sebastian's attentiveness. He hadn't tried to coerce her into anything low cut or ultra short. He'd bypassed all the dresses that might have made her uncomfortable and she appreciated his sensitivity.

The dress landed just above her knees and had a two-inch slit up one leg. It hugged what it covered, not tightly, just doing a lot to emphasize her slight figure. The front of the dress rose to her neck, but in the back, it dipped to her shoulder blades. Right now, Brandi could feel the warmth of Sebastian's fingers as they coasted over her skin. The man couldn't stop touching her, and she loved it.

She tried not to think about the coming night, because thinking of it made her queasy. She didn't want to mess things up by behaving like a ninny, or showing her cowardice. And she trusted him now, completely. But that didn't mean she'd be able to rest easy in his arms all night. If she had the nightmare, if she froze up and kept him awake, it would put a damper on their time together, and they only had a few days left.

The music ended and Sebastian smiled down at her. "What are you thinking about?"

He seemed in no hurry to leave the dance floor. That suited Brandi. Now that she felt comfortable dancing, she'd gladly do so all night—with Sebastian. "I was wondering about you. Where you live, if your work takes you away from home very often."

A guarded expression came over his face and he took her hand, leading her back to their table. After seating her, he asked, "Why so curious all of a sudden?"

Brandi didn't know where the questions had come from, or why. It was probably because she wanted to see more of him, in more normal circumstances, even though she knew that was impossible. Their time together seemed magical and unreal. In a way it *was* unreal because they were simply too different to form any lasting relationship. Sebastian was the most vital, energetic, appealing man she'd ever met.

And she was still a timid shadow of a woman. That wouldn't change, no matter how she wished it could.

"Brandi?"

He took her hand across the table—touching her again. She smiled to herself, loving the constant contact with him, and knowing she'd miss it once they returned home. But Sebastian deserved a whole woman, not one bogged down with emotional difficulties from her past.

"You know so much about me, but I don't even know where you live."

He seemed to consider that for a long moment before he answered. Brandi wondered if he thought she was prying, or if perhaps he wanted to keep his life separate so their parting at the end of the trip wouldn't be too complicated.

"I have an old farmhouse I've been renovating. To me, it's beautiful, filled with all natural woodwork and hardwood floors. It's how I spend much of my free time, working on the place. I had to replace a lot of the plumbing and the wiring. The roof was in horrible shape. But it has charm, and it's isolated, away from the congested suburbs and the busy city."

"Does it take you long to get to work each day?"

He shrugged. "That depends. My work differs from job to job, so I never know in which direction I'll be going, anyway. But it's about a forty minute drive to downtown, where I have my offices. There aren't any other houses around, and I own several acres, so my privacy will always be protected."

"That's important to you?"

He made a rough sound, not quite a laugh. "After growing up in tenement buildings where the hallways were always filled with loiterers, vagrants and drunks, and the front steps couldn't be walked on for the bodies resting there, yes, my privacy is damn important." His eyes narrowed on her, bright green and intense. "It's not something I'd ever be able to give up."

There was a warning there, or a message, but Brandi already knew their time was limited. She didn't need him to spell it out. "Do you spend a lot of time away from your home?"

"Occasionally. It's not uncommon for me to be gone for days at a time, but most of my jobs now are contained within the city." He tilted his head at her, as if trying to see into her thoughts. "I could limit my work out of town, if it ever became a problem."

Feeling uncomfortable now, because it was as if he knew she was asking for personal reasons, Brandi added, "I suppose for a single man, it isn't an issue."

"No. I've been expanding my offices, hiring on additional men for surveillance work. But it's a catch-22. Expansion will free up more of my time, but doing the expanding itself requires additional time and commitment."

Brandi couldn't imagine living in isolation, away from neighbors or friends and family. But she could tell by looking at Sebastian that it suited him. "So, you're happy there."

It wasn't a question, but a statement, and one more

obstacle to prove their time at the cabin was a fluke, not something that could be extended once the prize package had been used up.

"My home isn't fancy, but it's sturdy, and it's all mine. I enjoy being there, making the repairs myself, watching the house change. It's one of the few concessions with money that I made, buying my home. Buying the land. It's not easy for me to admit, but in a way the house is personal insurance on my security. I know I won't ever be broke and homeless, because I own it outright. And there's enough land to make a profit off any number of ventures if the need ever arose. Having money in the bank adds to security, but not like having a place that's free and clear to call your own. I know I won't ever end up like one of those vagrants sleeping on the front steps."

Brandi knew it was important to him for her to understand his financial independence. And in truth, she was amazed at how well he'd succeeded given his poor start in life. He didn't dress miserly, but neither did he wear exclusive brands or styles. His hair was kept neat—she loved his hair, so dark and straight and fine—but it wasn't salon styled. Brandi pictured him going to a local barber, and she smiled. "It's hard to imagine you worrying about money. You're successful and it shows. And you've been so generous with me."

He shrugged. "The dress wasn't all that expensive, though I admit I have no idea what women's clothes normally cost. Besides, I like seeing you in it. You look sexy as hell."

The thudding of her heart proved how his words affected her. But it wasn't just the compliment. It was that, in some small way, she'd succeeded in helping him overcome his reservations at needless spending. She wanted him to know he couldn't save the world, and there was certainly no crime indulging in a few luxuries for himself. "The dress is beautiful. Probably the nicest thing I've ever owned."

"If you like it, then it was worth ever penny."

She wished he could enjoy buying himself things as easily. "It's an extravagant gift." Then she grinned. "Especially since *you* were a gift, which I figured was plenty for one birthday."

His fingers tightened on hers. "I'm glad Shay chose me as the gift, not some other man."

"I'd have refused any other man." It was true. She'd taken one look at Sebastian and found his charm and strength and his smile irresistible. In her heart, she'd already chosen him, and Shay was astute enough to see it. "Besides, Shay had seen my interest in you—a unique thing for me—and I'd stupidly mentioned my new plans to her."

"Ah. I'd forgotten about that. What are these infamous plans of yours?"

Shrugging, Brandi said, "They're not really all that complex. I just want to get on with my life. I've hidden away long enough, and let the past mean more than it should. It just seemed easier to go it alone than to try to get beyond the problems. Especially when the men weren't exactly beating a path to my door. Not that I minded, since no man appealed to me anyway."

He gave her a crooked grin. "Until you saw me."

"Yes."

Leaning forward slightly, his expression now serious, he said, "I'd like to help with your plans if you'll let me."

"Oh, Sebastian." Impulsively, she lifted his hand to her mouth and kissed his knuckles. The action surprised him, but quickly the surprise changed to an emotion much hotter. His eyes blazed and his features tightened.

Brandi's voice trembled in reaction to that look. "When I said you were generous, I wasn't only talking about the dress. The dress is beautiful, and it was a wonderful gift, but you've given me yourself, too. You made it safe for me to find out things about myself and about lovemaking that I never would have known otherwise."

She no sooner said the words than she felt her face heat. "What we did wasn't exactly lovemaking, though, was it? It wasn't a shared thing, not with you doing all the giving and me doing all the taking."

He shook his head and his gaze held hers, not letting her look away. "Don't think of it like that. What happened today was incredible. *You* were incredible. So, it's not about me helping you. It's about me as a man wanting you as a woman. And finding a comfortable way for us to come together."

She wanted to believe him. But in her heart she knew

a man like Sebastian would never have been here with her in the first place if the circumstances hadn't dictated it. And once the vacation was over, she didn't know what would happen. She felt almost desperate at the thought of never seeing him again.

"I wish...I wish things could be normal between us. I wish I could give you as much as you've given me."

In one abrupt motion, Sebastian stood and pulled her to her feet. Startled, Brandi asked, "What are you doing?"

"I think it's time for us to go. I have some explaining to do, and a crowded restaurant isn't the place."

She went willingly as he pulled her out into the night air. It hadn't rained anymore, but the air was still thick with moisture, oppressive and heavy with the threat of another storm. Once inside the rental car, he turned to her and hauled her up against his chest.

Only vague moonlight spilled through the windows, leaving the interior of the car very dim. Brandi felt his hands tangling in her hair, pulling her even closer, and then his wonderful mouth covered hers and kissed her for long minutes.

He tasted hot and urgent. When she opened her mouth, his tongue pushed in, stroking and mating with her own. It was a familiar caress now. Many times while they'd been joined on the bed, Sebastian had demanded a kiss or a touch. She'd leaned over him, willing to obey him even though he'd been restrained. She'd let him excite her with his mouth, and kissing him now excited her again.

His lips moved over her cheek, her temple, then her ear. "You're making me crazy, honey."

She thrilled at the feel of his warm breath in her ear, the roughness of his shadowed jaw, and his use of endearments. They were a first for her, and she felt special each time he referred to her in such a way. "I'm sorry."

He groaned. "No, don't be. I like your unique brand of torment." He leaned back and gazed at her, his eyes hot in the dim light, his breathing audible. "I also like being tied down and tormented by you."

Brandi found it difficult to breathe with him looking at her so intently. "I didn't mean to torment you."

"God help me if you ever do mean it."

She saw the flash of his white grin, then he kissed her again, hard and hungry. His kisses, no matter how voracious, no longer frightened her.

"Men have fantasies just as women do," he whispered against her lips. "And I can safely say just about every male alive has fantasized being tied and helpless at the hands of a beautiful woman bent on sexual exploration. You didn't hurt me, you pleasured me, almost more than I could bear. Just thinking about it now is making me hard as granite."

Fascinated, Brandi remained stock-still while he kissed her once more. Her brain worked and when he lifted his mouth away, she asked, "What are your other fantasies?"

"Ah, curious are we?"

"Yes." She felt no embarrassment, not when he discussed things so openly and without shame. The heat of their bodies had caused the windows to steam up, and even if someone happened by, they were well hidden.

In a low gravelly tone, Sebastian said, "Some fantasies are purely sexual and damn basic." He named a few, and she knew her eyes were round with disbelief. She just hadn't ever imagined such things. Sebastian stroked her while he spoke, occasionally licking the sensitive spot beneath her ear, nipping her throat. His voice was deep and husky and aroused.

"Others are based more on emotion. Like being the protector of a woman, having her depend entirely on me for everything, including her pleasure."

"You'd like that?"

"Damn right."

"I thought men these days wanted independent women."

Sebastian chuckled. He kept kissing her, as if he couldn't help himself. They were quick, light kisses over her face, her hair, her throat and ears that teased and distracted.

"We're talking fantasies, Brandi, not real life. To the outside world, I wouldn't settle for anything less than an intelligent woman with a mind of her own. But in the bedroom, it's different. For both men and women. There, everyone has to find their own limits and explore different depths. There's no right or wrong. Only the truth of what turns them on. They have to be open and share their secrets to know what those truths are. We've done that, you know. And it was damn good."

"What other fantasies do you have?"

His big hand cupped her cheek and his thumb smoothed over her temple. "As much as I enjoyed being tied up, the thought of having a woman tied to my bed appeals a hell of a lot, too."

"I could never do that."

"And I'd never ask it of you. Fantasies are something given, not taken. If you didn't enjoy it, I wouldn't either."

Despite his reassurance, the panic was still there. She started to speak, but no words would come to her.

"Shhh. It's all right, babe. I wasn't suggesting it as an alternative. You asked and I answered. That's the thing about fantasies. They vary from person to person. So they don't always get met. But there are no bad fantasies, not between two consenting adults. Not between us."

She buried her face against his throat, feeling the heat in her cheeks—and in her body. Somehow, in some distant part of herself, the thought of being at this man's mercy had given her a tiny, forbidden thrill. She still wouldn't do it, because along with the thrill was the fear of being used and hurt. But she acknowledged the idea just the same.

"What about you, Brandi? Do you have any fantasies?"

She shook her head. She'd never given sex much

thought one way or the other—except to know she wanted to avoid it. "I don't think so."

"We'll find some fantasies for you. We still have three days left to work on it," he promised in a husky voice, and excitement filled her. Sebastian kissed her again, then turned and started the car. "We better get moving if I'm going to find a pharmacy that's open."

"Why are we going to a pharmacy?"

"I need to buy more condoms."

"Oh." That stifled her, but only for a moment. "I thought you said you just wanted to sleep with me tonight."

As he pulled the car away from the curb, he flashed her a boyish grin. "I do. Afterward."

Brandi kept silent, but on the inside, *she* was grinning, too.

9

LYING ON TOP OF Sebastian, feeling his wide chest heave with labored breaths, feeling the heat of his body waft around her, was something to which she'd quickly grown accustomed. His large hand still held her backside, massaging and squeezing. The man seemed to love her behind. She'd learned that he had a special fondness for that part of the female anatomy.

Brandi had a special fondness for him.

It hadn't taken him long to breach her reserves. After that first night of sleeping together, when she had slept more peacefully than she had in years, Brandi hadn't wanted to use her own room at all. Sebastian was always so careful of her, letting her have a dominant position in their lovemaking. They'd done away with the tethers after that one time. Though the ties still lay on the nightstand beside the bed, Sebastian hadn't mentioned using them, so Brandi hadn't either.

She no longer needed the security of physical binding, not when she trusted him so completely.

After the night of dancing, he'd taken her back to the cabin and begun kissing her as soon as they'd closed the front door. He'd carefully aroused her to where she couldn't see straight, then carried her to the bedroom where he arranged her over his big body and drove inside her.

The added stimulants of his hands and mouth being everywhere had been more than enough to chase away her fears. He never crowded her in bed, always putting Brandi on top. Like a puppet, she moved as he directed, trusting him to know what she would like, what would bring her pleasure. He never failed her.

More often than not, they slept that way afterward, her on top, his arms locked around her keeping her close.

Brandi knew her time with him was something she'd cherish forever, but she'd done the most ridiculous thing—she'd fallen in love with him. Five days ago she would have said a man like Sebastian didn't exist. Now, on their last day at the cabin, she had to admit that a man like him did exist, he just wasn't for her.

Sebastian stirred and she felt him lift his head to gently nip her shoulder. "What time is it?"

Brandi forced her eyes open to see the clock on the nightstand. "Four-thirty."

"You should get to sleep. We'll have to start packing up in a few hours."

His voice sounded gruff, and she wanted to cry. The past five days had been magical. They'd both been changed by the trip to some degree. She and Sebastian had gone shopping, where he'd helped her buy more gifts for everyone—and even a few souvenirs for himself. He didn't seem to mind so much now when he purchased something. He even seemed enthusiastic about it on occasion. Ice-cream cones, Ferris wheel rides, even having his fortune read. Small things, but they gave him enjoyment, and Brandi loved to see him relaxed and happy.

He'd volunteered to help her wrap all the gifts. They'd spent one entire rainy day in the cabin doing just that, then making love afterward in front of the fireplace.

He'd also given her everything she'd missed out on when growing up. He'd taken her parking to show her the dubious joys of making out in a car, and they'd laughed as much as they'd loved, especially when another car had come by and made them both think they'd been caught. He'd brought her wildflowers that now decorated the kitchen table in the cabin. Twice he'd carried her a tray so she could have her breakfast in bed. He'd pampered her and seduced her and wooed her. She loved him for it.

When the nightmare had come again two nights ago, he'd held her close while she struggled with her demons, and he listened while she talked. He hadn't made love to her then, he'd simply let her sleep in his arms. The nightmare had faded away quickly. Soothed by the rhythm of his heartbeat and the security of his touch, Brandi had to wonder if it would ever come again.

They both knew this was their last night, and Brandi clung to him for a moment. Sebastian's hands stilled, then he whispered, "Are you all right?"

"Hmm. I'm just not sleepy."

"Well..." He had that husky tone to his voice that told her he was aroused again. He amazed her with his stamina and his interest. She'd never before thought of herself as a sexual being, but with Sebastian she felt insatiable.

Rising up on her forearms she put her breasts within reach of him. He clasped her waist and moved her upward a bit more until he could carefully catch a nipple between his teeth. Brandi moaned.

"You have the most sensitive breasts."

"So you keep telling me."

"That's because it turns me on so much."

She was grateful that she could give him pleasure, because he'd certainly given it to her. Cupping his cheeks, she pulled him away from her breast and looked at him seriously. "I'd like to make you happy, Sebastian. This is our last night together."

He frowned, then caught her mouth in a ravenous kiss before saying, "I don't want to think about that right now."

She slid to the side of him, then surveyed his long body. With one finger trailing over his chest to his left nipple, she said, "What can I do for you?"

"Brandi..."

She loved his warning tone, the one that told her he liked very much what she was doing. She flicked his nipple, heard him hiss a breath past his teeth, then moved her hand down to his erection. "This part of your body fascinates me."

In rasping tones he admitted, "Your fascination drives me insane."

Brandi chuckled. Sebastian went still, not moving a muscle, and she hated that she caused him to do that, that he had to restrain himself now as much as the bonds ever had. Leaning down, she kissed his rigid stomach muscles, then dipped her tongue into his navel. He groaned brokenly.

"Do you know what I'd like to do?"

The groan turned into a choke. "I know what I'd like you to do."

"I'd like to go the lake."

Sebastian gave a raw laugh. "Aw, babe. You do know how to destroy a man, don't you?"

Brandi pretended not to hear him. She knew what he wanted, and so far she hadn't been daring enough to give it to him. But he'd sparked her curiosity, and she knew this might be her last chance to know all of him.

"I'd like to go to the lake and wrap up in a blanket with you. We could watch the stars and listen to the crickets and…make love."

His fingertips trailed up and down her spine. "Is this one of your fantasies, honey?"

"Yes, I think it is."

Sebastian had encouraged her to think of any fantasy she wanted, anything that appealed to her. And he'd made each and every one of them come true. But what he didn't understand was that the fantasies were all about him, not about time or place or position. Certainly not about any other person. And Brandi couldn't tell him, because she knew even though her fears seemed to have been put on hold, it was only because Sebastian was so careful with her.

He was a man, and how long would it be before the enforced caution bored him? Or worse, before he became annoyed with her and the restrictions? He deserved a woman as alive and open as himself, a woman unafraid to share herself in every way.

Not a woman with hang-ups that would eventually drive them apart.

Sebastian sat up and pulled Brandi into his lap. He nuzzled his whisker-rough cheek against her own soft cheek. "I can arrange this one, no problem. But are you sure you won't get cold?"

Sebastian seemed impervious to the chills that often affected her. She could be freezing, and he'd be comfortable. As he'd told her in the beginning, his body temperature was degrees higher than hers. She'd count on that temperature—and her own excitement—to keep her comfortable.

"It's been warm all day. I'll be fine. Let's just take some blankets. I want to stay to watch the sun come up."

The small lake was located close to their cabin. They'd been there several times while exploring, taking long walks and picking flowers and watching the occasional rabbit or squirrel. After that one night when Sebastian had spent a small fortune, Brandi tried to make certain they stayed close to the cabin. When they did go out—during her second shopping spree—she'd requested lunch at an inexpensive diner. Sebastian seemed to think she was accustomed to more luxury than she was. Like him, she lived a simple life, especially compared to Shay. The one picnic lunch they'd had at the lake had been her favorite meal of all. There just wasn't any way to convince Sebastian of that. He seemed intent on spoiling her, when it wasn't necessary at all.

Sebastian didn't complain as he pulled on jeans and a T-shirt, then gathered up quilts. Brandi put on her robe, tying the belt securely, but leaving herself naked beneath. If this was to be her last night with Sebastian, she intended to make the most of it. She could sleep anytime.

Sebastian was patient with her while she led the way to the lake. He even waited silently, his wide shoulders propped against a tree, while she took her time choosing a spot to spread the largest quilt. But when she untied the belt to her robe, he straightened.

"Brandi?"

The robe slid to the ground, leaving her naked in the pale moonlight. She'd never before so blatantly exposed herself for his view. Shyness had prevented her from being so bold, just as desperation now forced her to it. If this was to be her last night with him, she wanted everything, with no barriers between them.

There was no doubt he liked it. His gaze traveled over her in the shadows of the night, and she heard his low groan. Typical of Sebastian, though, he didn't move; he waited for her to direct him. Not once had he taken the control from her, which was probably why she'd been able to let loose as much as she had.

"Come here, Sebastian."

He kicked off his shoes and stepped into the center of the quilt with her. When he reached for her, Brandi took his hands, kissed each palm and then put them back at his sides. "Take your shirt off for me."

The shirt went over his head in record time. Brandi took it from him and laid it by her robe. She would have liked to completely undress him herself, but he was too tall for her to pull his shirt off. That was, however, the only concession she was willing to make. His jeans were very reachable.

She slid her cool fingers over the hard, heated skin of his abdomen, then under the first button of his fly. A soft breeze blew around them, bringing with it the scent of the lake, the azaleas and the dew-wet grass. The air was silent except for the rustle of leaves and their mingled breaths.

The first button slipped free. Brandi dropped to her knees and kissed the small patch of hair-rough skin she'd exposed. Sebastian sucked in his stomach on a startled breath.

The next button was a little more stubborn, but then the third and forth came undone with no difficulty. Sebastian hadn't bothered with briefs, and she could now circle the hot, hard length of his shaft with her hands. Brandi nuzzled his erection against her cheek.

His hand touched her head, then fell away. "Brandi," he groaned. "Honey, you're killing me."

She began working the jeans down his thighs to his knees. Her mouth trailed in the wake of her fingers, drifting over his inner thigh. "I love how you smell, Sebastian."

His hands hung in fists at his sides. In a strangled rasp, he asked, "How do I smell?"

"Warm and musky. Sexy. Very male."

"Brandi, why don't we lie down now?"

"No. Not yet." She wanted this night to be special to him, and she wanted it to be enough to carry her for the rest of her life. There would never be another man like Sebastian. He'd given her back herself, shown her how to be a woman again. But she'd never be woman enough to keep him happy. Though she loved him, he deserved so much more than she could give.

The thought caused her heart to ache, but she banished reality by leaning forward and drawing him deep into her mouth.

Sebastian cursed and groaned and for one instant, his hand tangled almost painfully in her hair. Brandi started to pull back, fearing he'd lost control, but he released her and locked his hands behind his neck.

"Sebastian?"

He panted. "Sweetheart, what you're doing... I like it very much."

Brandi licked her lips, still tasting him. "If I do it wrong..."

He laughed, a hoarse sound of disbelief. "There is no wrong way, babe. Not between me and you. Just please don't quit on me."

"No. I won't do that." Then she leaned forward. "Do you like this?" She licked the very tip of him and heard him gasp. "And this?" Her mouth slid slowly down the length of him until she couldn't take any more into her mouth. Sebastian's only answer was a broken moan.

She realized there was another fantasy she wanted to fulfill, and she went about working toward that end. She knew her movements were awkward, but he didn't complain. Far from it. He begged and cursed and praised. And finally, after his entire body had started to tremble in taut expectation, he pulled away from her and quickly kicked free of his jeans.

"Sebastian?"

Swearing, he knelt down and dug in his pocket until he found a condom, but his hands shook too badly to put it on, and Brandi took it from him. She hadn't finished what she'd started, but she wanted him too much to quibble. Deftly sliding the condom over his swollen member, she reacted to his urgency. Sebastian heaved beside her, and his hands were hard as they grabbed her around the waist and lifted her onto his lap. He drove into her with one smooth, powerful thrust, and came almost simultaneously. Brandi was so excited herself, knowing she'd driven him to such a degree of desire, she only had to continue to move on him a half minute before she too exploded, then slumped against his chest.

Long minutes passed in silence while they held each other, and Brandi wondered if Sebastian, too, was already feeling the loss. She didn't want to go back, but she knew it was inevitable. She had a job and a family. He had his work and his house.

She'd never get to see his house, she realized. In her mind, she'd pictured it, how it would look, how it might be improved even more with a woman's touch. Only she would never be that woman.

Surely they would run into each other again. After all, he was a friend of Shay's, helped her with the shelter, and Brandi spent much of her time with Shay working on getting donations and assistance for the shelter.

But when she did see him, she wouldn't cause a scene. She'd be mature, and friendly. Never would she make him regret his generosity. Never would she make him uncomfortable for having given himself to her.

They spent the rest of the morning at the lake, not talking, just holding each other. And when the sun came up, Brandi did her best not to hate the coming day. Sebastian kept her warm, wrapped in his heat and a blanket. Just as dawn broke, he made love to her again. It was probably just her heart breaking, but his movements seemed as desperate as her own.

Three hours later, they caught a plane for home.

WITH EACH PASSING SECOND, Sebastian grew angrier. Damn it, how could everything just end as if none of it had ever happened? Yet that was evidently what Brandi wanted. On the plane, she'd distanced herself from him, only holding his hand during takeoff and landing. She'd even suggested they take separate rides home, to save him the time of going by her house. Luckily, Shay had sent the limo after them, giving him a good excuse to refuse her offer.

He'd wanted to shout then, but he'd held himself back. Hell, he'd been holding himself back from the start. She didn't even know him, because he hadn't wanted to hurt her, hadn't wanted her to be disappointed by the fact that she'd given herself to him. He also hadn't wanted the Gatlinburg trip to be the end of their relationship.

Several times he'd started to tell her how he felt, only to draw up short. It probably had something to do with the poor kid still in him, but he didn't want to risk her rejection. She'd had a whole new world opened up to her, and she deserved a chance to explore that world. On the other hand, everything basic and primal in him demanded he claim her, that he make her understand she belonged to him and only him. He tried to convince himself it was only the erotic sexual circumstances of their time together that was making him feel so territorial. But he'd been with plenty of women, and he'd never felt this way before.

He knew it would never happen again.

She hadn't asked to see him, hadn't mentioned furthering their relationship. For Brandi, it seemed to be over with already, and she wasn't even home yet.

He felt the tension building with each mile that passed. He had to do something before he lost his head and transformed into a barbarian. Turning to Brandi, he asked, "Will Shay be coming by to see you?"

She sent him a small smile. "No doubt. She's probably waiting on my doorstep."

Sebastian wondered if Brandi would tell Shay about them. Not that it would matter. Brandi was her own woman, independent despite her reserve. He remembered first meeting her—it seemed like months ago, rather than days. She'd been adamant and outspoken in her desire *not* to go anywhere with him. She hadn't wanted him, not even as part of a luxurious prize package. She had no trouble leading her own life.

She'd only needed him for sex.

He'd given her that, even though their intimacy had been controlled. It should have been enough, should have been the ultimate fantasy, but now it made him feel empty. Rather than being anxious to get back to his house, and to the job he loved, he dreaded each minute that passed. It put him one minute closer to losing her.

He cleared his throat, trying to chase the panic away. "When will you go to the shelter?"

"First thing tomorrow. I can't wait to give the kids their presents."

He forced a smile. "I'm sure they'll be excited."

"I appreciate all the help you gave me, picking out the gifts and wrapping them."

"I enjoyed myself."

Brandi hesitated, her hands twisted together in her lap. "Sebastian..."

Hoping to hear an invitation, some clue as to how she felt, he held his breath and waited.

"I want you to know how much this trip has meant to me."

The anger hit him, but he controlled it. Trying not to sound sarcastic, he said, "No problem. It wasn't exactly painful for me."

Brandi looked confused, her gaze darting over his face, then away. Her voice dropped and he heard a slight tremor in the tone that hadn't been there moments before. "It was very special to me. And I'll never forget it."

He'd hurt her feelings and now he despised himself for it. Damn her new freedom, her rights. Yes, she deserved some time to sort out her feelings, but that didn't mean he wanted to let her go cold like this. He put his arm around her and tugged her closer to his side. Her face turned up to his, her expression wary, and he whispered, "We're...friends, babe. I hope you'll call me if you ever need to talk or visit."

She blinked, looking pleasantly surprised by his offer, and she gave him a shaky smile.

Then he added, "Or if you ever need this." And his mouth closed over hers. He didn't care if the limo driver watched, he didn't care if the whole world saw them.

Brandi's fingers dug into his shoulders, not to push him away, but to hold him close. His tongue slid along her lips, then inside. He ate at her mouth, devouring, consuming. He wanted her to remember him, he wanted her to realize this was special, not something she'd find with any other man.

Not something she could toss away.

He pressed her back against the seat and heard her soft moan as his fingers found and toyed with her nipple through her dress. He wanted her in his mouth. He wanted her naked beneath him.

He wanted her.

Realization came slowly, but the stillness finally penetrated his brain. The limo had stopped. Sebastian lifted his head and he scanned the area. Brandi's house. It was over.

He looked at her and saw her damp parted lips, her eyes still closed. With a gentle kiss he whispered, "You're home, Brandi."

Her thick lashes lifted and she gazed at him a moment before comprehending. "Oh." She tried to straighten herself and Sebastian couldn't help but smile as she tucked dark curls behind her ears and they immediately sprang forward again to frame her face. He loved her hair. Loved her face. He loved everything about her.

The driver had been busy unloading Brandi's bags from the trunk. He carried them up to her front steps and Sebastian started to get out to help. She caught his hand and stopped him.

"I'd rather say goodbye right here."

He settled back into his seat, staring at her hard. He couldn't let her go like this, not without giving her fair warning. He wouldn't commit himself, but he had to at least let her know things weren't over, no matter what she thought.

"For the past five days, I've let you call the shots, Brandi. And I don't regret one second of it. But the trip is over and from now on, I'm playing by my own rules."

Her eyes widened and her voice was weak. With arousal? "I don't understand."

Sebastian grinned. Having made up his mind to take the decision away from her, he felt much better. Patience no longer suited him well. "Sure you do." He cupped her cheek and smoothed his thumb over her kiss-swollen lips. "There is no goodbye, Brandi. Not between us. You may not realize that yet. But you will. Soon."

She stared at him in confusion and, if he didn't miss his guess, excitement. Then she scurried from the limo and hurried up the walk to her front door. Sebastian watched her, waiting. At the last moment, she turned to look back at him.

He'd give her twenty-four hours to think about things. Then he was staking his claim. Maybe he was a barbarian, after all.

10

"ALL RIGHT, SHAY, where is she?"

Shay bit her bottom lip, but her back was straight and she was so tall she nearly looked him in the eye. "I can't tell you."

He cursed, a colorful, explicit curse that had Shay lifting her beautiful eyebrows and pursing her lips.

Sebastian was at the end of his tether. He'd meant to give Brandi one day to get settled back at home, to get accustomed to the idea that he intended to pursue their relationship. But he'd gotten called away on a case, one he couldn't hand to anyone else because he'd been previously involved and knew the history. As much as he'd wanted to see Brandi, he had obligations that he couldn't ignore—not when it came to a woman being stalked by her ex. The woman couldn't afford to hire anyone else, and Sebastian already understood the situation. He'd wanted to call Brandi beforehand, but it had been so late. And by the time he'd gotten back, none of his calls got answered.

Now, a week later, he still couldn't reach her and his anger had grown steadily with each passing hour. He'd had more time away from her than with her, and the thought nettled him. So even though it was the dinner hour, and he might have been intruding, he'd gone to Shay's house. He wanted answers, and she was the only one who might be able to give them to him.

"You're playing some game here, Shay, and I don't like it. I need to talk to Brandi. Tell me where she is."

"I'm sorry, Sebastian, really. But she made me promise."

"Why?"

At that point Shay lost her temper. With one finger poked into his chest, she stood on her tiptoes and looked him dead in the eye. She shouted, "That's what I'd like to know! What the hell did you do to my sister? She hasn't been the same since she came back. One minute she looks ready to burst into tears, then she's smiling like she has some damn secret to keep, and then she informs me she needs a vacation! She just came back from Gatlinburg! She won't tell me a single thing that happened there."

"Maybe because it's none of your business."

"We share everything!"

"Even guilt?"

Shay went still, her eyes wide. "What are you talking about?"

Sebastian regretted the words as soon as they'd left his mouth. There was no point in rehashing the past. It wouldn't solve anything, and in fact, might make matters worse. He intended to be around from now on, and he'd make certain things changed, that her family understood Brandi better.

He needed to divert Shay, and he sighed. "Do you

intend to leave me standing in the doorway, or can I come in and sit down? I'm beat."

Her frown softened, and then she sighed, too. "Come on. We can go into my study and talk there."

Sebastian looked around in amazement as he entered Shay's home. Luxurious, rich, expansive—all the things he'd expected but seeing them now made his gut twist. How could he ask Brandi to come to his modest home when she had this in her family?

"It's a great house," he said when he noticed Shay watching him.

"It's an empty house and terribly lonely at times." She opened a thick oak door to a large parlor done in rich shades of burgundy and hunter green. "Brandi has no use for it. She thinks I ought to buy something more homey. She calls it a depressing mausoleum."

Sebastian stared hard at Shay, wondering at her words and how much truth was behind them. "Brandi actually said that?"

Shay nodded, looking around the room with a poignant half smile. "And I'd even agree with her, except that this is where my husband chose to live, and since his death this is all I have left of him. Besides, after a while, the place kind of grows on you."

Shay was such a young, beautiful, vital woman, it was often difficult to think of her as a widow. He reached out and gave her hand a quick squeeze. "I'm sorry."

He'd said it before, countless times to countless victims. It always felt less than adequate and left him feeling hollow, as it did now.

Shay ran her fingertips over a mahogany desk, and Sebastian could see the memories in her eyes. "Don't be. I'm content with my life and the choices I've made. But I want Brandi to be happy, too, and something just isn't right with her."

He scrubbed his hand over his tired eyes. Shay looked unhappy as hell, her worry plain to see, and he decided right then he wouldn't tell her how she'd innocently added to Brandi's burden. It wouldn't happen again, because he'd be there, making certain it didn't.

He intended to make Brandi happy, and to keep her that way, so the point was now moot. "I didn't mean to let this much time pass before seeing her again, but I was called away. I just got back in town this morning. I tried calling her twice while I was gone, and several times since I've been home, but I couldn't get an answer."

"She was probably avoiding you."

Well, that was typical of Shay to be so blunt. Sebastian dropped into a chair and leaned his head back. "I ought to strangle you for getting me into this mess."

"Is that what it is? A mess?"

"What the hell would you call it? You send me off on an innocent trip...only it wasn't so innocent."

"Uh, I hesitate to ask, but what exactly are you telling me?"

He couldn't help but laugh. "Not what you think. I

was supposed to entertain your sister for five days, but instead, I fell in love with her in one. The rest of the trip was pure torture, and even though I kept telling myself she deserved a second chance at life without a possessive Neanderthal like myself hanging around, I can't just let her go."

Shay blinked twice. "You love Brandi?"

His voice softened at her amazement and he said simply, "How could I not?"

Shay's smile was blinding. "Exactly! She's perfect, isn't she?"

"No, she's beautifully flawed and I want her. Where is she, Shay?"

"It might not be that easy. You see, I get the impression Brandi doesn't think she's good enough for you."

That volatile anger roiled in his stomach, giving him cramps. It was worse than worrying about money, because Brandi made him feel more secure, more valued, than money ever could. He contemplated Shay's statement, and his eyes narrowed. "Where did she get that harebrained idea?"

"From you evidently, so you can just stop glaring daggers at me. Right now, Brandi thinks you walk on water. To hear her tell it, you're the perfect man."

Emotion swelled inside him—pride and need and lust. "She said that?"

"Not the part about you being too good for her. I just figured that out on my own, given the solemn way she sang your praises. Let me see, you're gentle and confident and understanding and caring and... Oh, yeah.

Strong." Shay punched his shoulder and winked. "But then any woman with a pulse can see that on her own."

"You're a terror, Shay. When you snag a man, he'd better have a will of iron so you don't trample him into the mud."

"Ha! Been there, done that. I have no intention of getting involved—much less married—ever again."

"Spoken like a woman on the brink of a great fall."

Shay made a rude sound. "I'm too sturdy to fall. Brandi's the one who's fallen, and I want to know what you're going to do about it."

All traces of fatigue left him. He'd spent four days in surveillance, two in wrapping up an attempted assault which he physically prevented. The ex-girlfriend of the assailant had bordered on hysteria, and it had taken him a long time to calm and reassure her. He'd been on and off planes for more hours than he cared to count, and he'd had nothing but broken, disturbed sleep on any given night. An hour ago he'd felt bruised, physically and mentally tired, and ready to collapse. But now his anger made him ready to burst with adrenaline. He needed an outlet, and Brandi with all her stubbornness seemed like a prime target.

How dare she think she wasn't good enough for him?

He stood to tower over Shay and his tone emerged as a low, mean growl. "I'm going to take care of everything. As soon as you tell me where she is."

Shay backed up. "I know you're inclined to be a little autocratic on occasion. And I appreciate the fact that with your job, it's probably necessary. But you aren't going to do anything...well...uncivilized, are you?"

He snorted. Shay knew him well enough she shouldn't have been worried at all. "I'm going to make your irritating little sister see reason, that's all." *After* he made love to her a couple of dozen times. When he'd finished, she'd know for certain just how much she meant to him.

Shay grinned and patted his arm. "I'll get you the address." She went around her desk to open the top drawer. "But I'm counting on you to make this work out, Sebastian. I don't want to have to deal with Brandi's temper if she comes back here alone."

"She's not going anywhere without me."

"Ohhh. A forceful man. Be still my heart." She fanned her face with a small square of white paper.

Sebastian grabbed the slip of paper from her hand. "Ha. You're too damn bossy to ever put up with a forceful man and you know it. You'd have him begging for mercy within twenty-four hours."

Shay shrugged. "Damn right. But I can have my fantasies."

As he started out, he said over his shoulder, "Yeah, we all do." And Brandi was about to fulfill his, whether she liked it or not.

BRANDI STEPPED OUT onto the front porch of the small rental cabin, and opened her arms to the feeling of being wrapped in a big black sky filled with diamonds. There wasn't a cloud in sight to block the stars and the moon was a fat orb that glowed softly. She wondered if this was how Sebastian felt when he stood in the isolation of his own home; at peace, lulled by his surroundings. Then she felt keen regret, because she would never know.

This cabin was rustic compared to the elegant one she'd shared with Sebastian. She preferred it here, though, if she had to be alone, because this cabin had a gentle familiarity to it, a hominess that she needed to mend her broken heart.

He hadn't called. He hadn't come to see her.

Though she knew it was for the best, for a short time she'd hoped for more. Sebastian had seemed so determined to continue their relationship, that a secret part of her had hoped he would force the issue, that he would take her choices away. But then those first few days had passed and she hadn't heard from him. After that, she'd accepted what was right for both of them.

Still, she missed him terribly. Everything she did, everywhere she looked, she thought of him. The nights were the worst. There wasn't a repeat of the nightmare, just the endless loneliness, and the knowledge of what she was missing. It had only been five days—the same length of time as the mundane workweek she usually put in—but time enough for her to fall completely, irrevocably in love.

It wasn't a mere infatuation with her first lover; no infatuation could be this strong, this all consuming. She had no doubts about the depth of her feelings. She loved him, and that wasn't going to go away.

It was Sebastian she had to wonder about. Was it possible for a man to be so gentle and considerate and not be emotionally involved? Could he have been using the situation only to gratify them both sexually? He'd always had her best interests at heart, she knew that as well as she knew her own limitations. Sebastian hadn't used her. But he'd admitted the circumstances were a fantasy for him, for almost any man. And what normal, healthy man would turn down the invitations she'd given? Now that the trip was over, maybe he'd decided to find a woman with fewer inhibitions, someone who could meet his high level of sexuality without faltering.

Moving to sit in an old wooden rocker, she closed her eyes and immediately the fantasies began to intrude. She had never considered fantasizing about a person before, but Sebastian had been so open about it, so natural, that his fantasies were now her own. In her mind, she could clearly see his bare, powerful body drawn taut on the bed, his expression hard and heated as she gently, endlessly rode him. The sounds of pleasure he made, the way his breath rasped, the thrusting of his hips as he struggled against his bonds. A tingle started inside her, and she felt the ache more keenly than ever.

She knew now what she was missing, and the knowing hurt. But she wouldn't have gone back to her ignorance for anything, her memories of the time with him were too precious to regret.

Disgusted with herself and her obsession with a man

she couldn't have, she started to rise. An unfamiliar sound made her hesitate; tires crunched on the long gravel drive, then braked to the side of the house. With her entire body straining with the effort, she listened to the sound of a car door slamming, the noise carried easily on the still night air.

No one knew she was here, so she certainly didn't expect any visitors. Unless Shay had come to check on her, which was possible. But the stomping footsteps that rounded the house weren't made by a woman, and just that quickly, all her old fears returned, choking her, slowing her heartbeat. She was alone, vulnerable....

A familiar figure bounded onto the porch and Sebastian stood there, overwhelmingly big and strong, making the small porch seem even smaller. Relief, yearning, confusion—they all swamped her at once. She sat frozen, unsure what to do, how to react. He didn't notice her sitting so quietly in the corner. He had his hands on his hips and a fierce frown on his face. To Brandi's eyes, he looked incredibly gorgeous.

Then one large fist raised to pound on her door. In the next instant, he bellowed her name in demand, the sound echoing dully around them. Brandi had no doubt he was angry.

She spoke quietly from her shadowed corner. "What are you doing here?"

He whirled toward her, his eyes searching in the darkness. When he located her, he stepped close. He wrapped his long fingers firmly around her upper arms and half lifted her from the chair.

"I came for you. Why the hell are you hiding from me?"

"Hiding?" His tone was antagonistic, almost brutal. Brandi didn't understand his mood at all.

"Yes, damn it. I've been trying to reach you. I had to threaten Shay to find out where you were."

He had frightened her half to death coming out here this way, and now he accused her? In the week since they'd parted, she'd suffered ten kinds of hell, missing him, wanting him. *Needing him.* And he verbally attacked with his first breath. She tried to pull away from him, but he held firm, so she did her best to stare him in the eyes. She had to tip her head way back to do so. "I'm not hiding, you big jerk. I'm relaxing. And why shouldn't I have gone away? You said you were going to call, but then you didn't."

She hadn't meant to make that accusation. It served no purpose, except to show the measure of her hurt. Pride made her stiffen. As much as she wanted him, she wouldn't humiliate herself.

Muttering, she said, "Shay should have kept her mouth shut. She promised me."

"Yeah, well she buckled under my threats."

Brandi snorted. "Shay doesn't buckle under to anyone."

"Okay, so she was more reasonable than you." He shook her gently, and his tone was urgent. "I explained to her I was called out of town on an emergency, and she believed me."

"You were out of town?"

He made a rough sound of exasperation. "*Yes*. I had to deal with a case where only I knew the history. I couldn't hand it over to anyone else."

Just looking at him made her heart beat faster. She licked her lips, more aware than ever of the differences in their heights, their strengths. "Was it a woman you had to help?"

He ran a hand through his hair. "Yeah. But it's over for good now. The jerk harassing her had a prior of petty theft. This time he had robbed a small convenience store. They had him on film. After she contacted me, I got the police involved and we set him up. The damn fool tried shooting at the cops."

Brandi swayed, and automatically she reached out to touch the solid strength of his chest, verifying that he was still in one piece. "You could have been hurt."

He shook his head. "I'm fine."

For the first time, she noticed the exhaustion in his eyes, apparent even in the dim moonlight. Being a hero was tiring work. Yet he'd come after her. Tears clouded her vision and she didn't know what to think.

All the differences between them had never seemed more magnified. He was close to a Superman figure, but she was certainly no Lois Lane.

"I tried to call once I got settled in a hotel, but you didn't answer your phone."

"The phone rang really late a couple of times. I

thought it was Shay. She's driving me nuts, wanting to coddle me, and at the same time trying to pry details out of me. She's not being at all subtle."

Sebastian's grin shone very white in the darkness. "I'm relieved that's all it was. Shay told me you were avoiding me."

This time, she really would strangle Shay once she got home. "No, I wasn't doing that." Then she shrugged. "I didn't think there was any reason to avoid you. You hadn't called. I thought it was over."

His fingers tightened on her arms, not hurting her, but letting her feel his strength. "No."

That one word held a wealth of determination. Very carefully, Brandi pulled away from him. Not because she was afraid, but because she needed time to think. She stepped behind the rocker. "Sebastian, I'm sorry if I misunderstood. But it was for the best anyway. We can't continue where we left off."

"Bullshit."

Shocked, Brandi curled her fingers over the wooden slats of the chair. Her anger simmered. "I'm trying to be honest here," she shouted in frustration.

"Then be honest and admit you want me! I'm too damn tired for more games."

Knowing she was only reacting to his anger, Brandi tried to find a measure of calm, but she couldn't. Sebastian was simply being too brutally provoking. "We're not suited to each other," she insisted.

"I'll warn you right now, honey," he said, his tone hard and low and rasping, "if you give me any nonsense about not being good enough for me, you probably won't like the consequences."

"I'll always have the fears, Sebastian, and eventually, they'll come between us!"

He cursed again, loudly, and Brandi's temper rose to match his. "Quit cursing at me! Do you think this decision has been easy for me? I'm trying to do what's best for both of us. So go home and leave it alone." Tears stung her eyes. In disgust, Brandi turned away and stomped into the house. Sebastian followed.

With only one light on in the tiny kitchenette, the interior of the cabin was dim. "Don't walk away from me, Brandi." He caught her arm and swung her around. Lowering his face close to hers, he said, "I've given you as much space as I can. From the very first, you've wrapped me around your little finger. But I'll be damned if I'll let you end it this easy. *I care about you.*"

Brandi had given this a lot of thought, and she was prepared to be reasonable, even noble, despite the volatile mood. She squared her shoulders and stated, "Sebastian, you're a hero."

With a hoot of rough laughter, he sneered and said, "Is this a new fantasy, Brandi? Hey, I'm game, you know that. But I need to know the details if you want me to play the right role."

He looked dangerous, and Brandi imagined this was how he looked when he worked. He seemed poised to jump on her, but she knew he wouldn't. She trusted him. Still, her own anxiety made her tone as harsh as his. "Damn it, Sebastian, will you just listen?"

He looked ready to snarl in anger, but finally he nodded.

Brandi drew a steadying breath, but she couldn't calm herself. The truth of what she was losing, of what she was chasing away, made her angry. "You've been rescuing women for years, starting with your mother, then in your business. You've always seen women as small and vulnerable. Being a protector is as much a part of you as your sexuality."

His low growl reverberated in the quiet cabin. "I don't think of women as inferior people, Brandi."

"I know you don't." She tried to keep her voice even, desperate to make him understand. Still, her words came too fast and too hard. "The reality of your size and strength in comparison to a woman's is obvious in everything you do. And more than most men, you're aware of that reality. It's ingrained in you, with your job, your background. And you...you probably viewed me, with the circumstances of my rape, as a woman in more need of rescuing than most."

He shook his head. "I wasn't initiating a rescue attempt when I let you tie me down. I was answering a sexual need. I was hot, and you were the answer."

Brandi took a step forward, her eyes narrowed. He was deliberately being crude, trying to embarrass her. In low tones, she said, "Good. Because you don't have to rescue me. The five-day fling is over. Your obligation is over."

His snarl was loud and ferocious. "Damn you! Is that all you think it was? An *obligation?* I've got plenty of obligations, lady, but I don't usually handle them in bed."

Brandi felt her cheeks heat, but refused to look away from him. "Our situation was unique."

"Damn right it was. You used me, and now you're through, is that it?"

Her breath caught painfully. *"No!"*

"Listen to me, Brandi, and listen good." He still frowned, but now his expression was intent, filled with cold determination. "My house will never be fancy, nothing like Shay's, but it's mine, and it's not something I can give up. Anything else is negotiable but that. I have enough money put away that you can redecorate as many times as you like. And I've already decided to limit the cases that take me out of town. The house is isolated, but you won't be alone there very often. I'll even hire a maid, if that'll make you feel better. It's not a mansion, but you'll adjust."

Tears blinded her, and without thinking she struck him hard in the chest. It felt like hitting a stone wall, and she gasped with the pain of it, cradling her hand to her chest. Sebastian blinked, his anger replaced by surprise, but other than that, he didn't show any sign that the blow had registered.

Brandi went on tiptoe to try to look him in the eyes. "Damn you, Sebastian, this isn't about money! It isn't about a house or maids or decorating. It's about *you*."

She tried to strike him again, and this time he caught

her fist and held it against his chest. "Stop that. You're going to hurt yourself."

Brandi snarled with her anger. "I don't care about money!"

"But I do. A little too much."

"Ha! What about the cases you don't charge for? You made it sound like it was an isolated case here and there, but Shay told me there were a lot of people who needed you, and you do the work gratis."

He stiffened, as if he didn't want that part of his life examined too closely. "Not everyone with a need has that kind of money to spend. I make a more than sufficient income on the bigger cases."

"That's exactly my point! You don't hoard your money. You're not oblivious to those in need. God, you're the most generous man I've ever known."

"Brandi…"

"No! You listen to me this time. I love you, you big jerk. You're an amazing man, considerate and sexy and strong and gentle and…" She faltered, the words choking her. She cleared her throat and stared up at him. "You can have any woman you want, Sebastian. You don't need me."

His eyes suddenly blazed with a savage expression. *"Like hell I don't."*

"Sebastian…"

"I need you and I want you." He jerked her up against his hard, hot body. "Right now."

She glared and actually stomped her foot. "You are *not* going to sidetrack me with sex!"

Sebastian caught both of her wrists and used them to control her, holding her just tight enough to let her know she couldn't escape him. A slow grin suddenly spread over his face. "You are so damn beautiful."

Brandi gasped. "Aren't you listening to me? Have you heard a word I've said? This would never work out between us. You deserve everything a woman has to offer. But I can't give it to you, because part of me is forever gone. You deserve so much more than I can— Umpf!"

Sebastian jerked her hard into his body and his mouth muffled her protests. He kissed her, letting her feel his anger, his lust. When he pulled away, Brandi was dazed.

"I warned you not to do that, not to put yourself down. Don't you ever belittle yourself, do you hear me?" He kissed her again, a quick hard kiss, then whispered, "I love you, Brandi. I accept all your flaws, just as I hope you'll accept all of mine. Having you makes me feel more secure than any amount of money ever could. And you might as well know right now, I'm never letting you go."

Before Brandi could form a coherent argument—if indeed she would have—Sebastian picked her up and carried her to the only bedroom. It housed a double bed, and as he lowered her to the mattress, his mouth came down on hers again, stifling any complaint she might have made. Brandi struggled against him, especially when he started pulling off her T-shirt. Nothing had been settled yet!

He misunderstood and said against her lips, "It's just me, babe. Only me." His head lowered to her breast and he sucked her nipple gently into the heat of his mouth. Brandi arched up off the mattress with a harsh cry of pleasure.

Lowering his full weight onto her to keep her still, Sebastian trailed his mouth over her breasts, kissing the other nipple, then moving down to her ribs. Brandi writhed beneath his comforting weight, loving the feel of him over her, surrounding her. Her earlier fantasies, combined with his sudden appearance and her raw emotions, left no room for anything other than need. She could no longer focus on fear, regrets, or what might be right or wrong for the future.

Sebastian growled and his hand slid between her thighs, seeking, probing. He didn't hold back now, didn't temper his desire or his urgency. Brandi moaned.

"I need you, babe. Right now."

"*Yes.*" Brandi said the word mindlessly, her hips lifting into his, pressing. He unsnapped her shorts and jerked them open. His long fingers caught at the waistband, and he stripped her shorts down her legs, taking her panties with them. Sitting poised between her widespread legs, he looked at her. The heat in his eyes should have brought on her wariness, but instead, it thrilled her.

He was back, and he wanted her. He'd said he loved her.

"Sebastian?"

"I'm sorry, sweetheart, but I can't wait."

Brandi screamed when his mouth pressed against her sensitive flesh. His tongue touched and explored; he suckled and nipped with his sharp teeth, and through it all, he held her legs spread wide with his rough hands. Brandi had almost no time to adjust to the unfamiliar caresses before she felt her climax building. Her body arched high, pressing her closer to his mouth, closer.... She felt suspended with intense pleasure for long seconds before the feelings began to diminish.

When she slumped into the mattress, her breathing still harsh and her heart thundering against her ribs, Sebastian leaned back and quickly fumbled with his belt and the closure of his slacks. The zipper came down and he eased the restriction of clothing away from his erection.

Balancing on his arms above her, he positioned himself, then gently probed against her slick folds. He made a low sound of pleasure. "You feel so hot and wet." He slid in an inch, pacing himself, then squeezed his eyes closed. "Tight."

Brandi wrapped her legs around him. She loved him. And she needed him now. *Sebastian.*

He thrust forward, and this new position, with him planted firmly between her thighs, left her helpless to counter his thrusts. The sense of being totally vulnerable to him—feeling him so deeply inside her, stretching her—enhanced her pleasure rather than inhibiting it. They both groaned.

When he gruffly apologized, Brandi knew he had meant to be slow and gentle. But their mating had turned urgent. Unlike the lovemaking that Brandi had controlled, this was wild and primal, and so beautiful she cried.

Within minutes, she came again, but it was better this time, the feelings more intense, deeper, because Sebastian was a part of her. She wrapped herself around him and screamed with her pleasure. Sebastian's low growl followed, while his shoulders tensed and his hips pumped wildly. Then he slumped onto her, his body limp, sated.

Brandi drew her fingers up and down the long expanse of his back, solid with muscle, warm and damp from his sweat. She loved him, every big gorgeous inch of him, from his hair-rough legs to his whiskered chin. He was the most incredible man, and if she could believe his words, he was hers.

Smiling, she said, "You were wrong."

He stiffened, then carefully levered himself upward. Brandi felt tears sting her eyes at his look of uncertainty. She raised her head enough to kiss him, letting her lips play lightly over his. "You told me I wouldn't like the consequences—but I liked them very much."

Sebastian grinned, then dropped his forehead to hers. "I love you, Brandi. Don't ever leave me again."

"I won't. Not if you really love me."

"I love you so much it terrifies me."

Everything seemed perfect, but she had to make certain. "The nightmares might not be gone."

"Nothing that emotional is ever completely gone. I'll always have a soft spot for people in need, and feel sickened by financial waste. I'll always take part in charities, needing to help as much as I can. Things become part of us, molding us, making us the people we are. Good and bad, we just have to adjust and be who we are."

"I love who you are, your scruples, your dedication, your morality. I think you're a wonderful person."

"I love you, too. We'll deal with anything that comes up. Together."

He kissed her, long and sweet, then not so sweet. "I forgot to use a condom."

Brandi chuckled at his chagrin. "Is your house big enough for a baby or two?"

His eyes turned a fierce, bright green. "Yeah, it's plenty big enough. And there are trees in the yard that would be perfect for a playhouse, or a tire swing. And a creek around the back of the property where we could catch crawdads and minnows and tadpoles."

The tears overflowed her eyes, but she managed a wobbly smile. "I'd say it sounds like life with you will be perfect."

He cupped her face. "Will you marry me?"

"I think Shay would probably insist on it."

He chuckled. "And if Shay wasn't around to force the issue?"

Widening her eyes in mock alarm, she asked, "You're not thinking of doing anything nefarious with my sister, are you?"

"No way. I owe Shay big for setting us up together in the first place." He pushed his hips against her, reminding her that he was still inside her—and aroused once more. "Now, will you answer me?"

She moaned, her eyes closing as his gentle thrusts stole her thoughts.

"Brandi?"

"Yes, I'll marry you. Just please don't stop what you're doing."

Sebastian grinned past his own desire. He slid one hand between their bodies, finding her heat and making her moan loudly. Now that he'd been partially sated, and the desperate need to get a commitment from her had been appeased, he could take it a little easier, go a little slower. Tease a little more.

Brandi looked beautiful with her incredible dark hair wild around her face, her lips parted, her cheeks flushed. She wanted him and she no longer felt any shyness in admitting her need. He kissed her nipple and felt her internal muscles squeeze him.

"Brandi?" he whispered, his lips against her soft skin. "Did I ever tell you the fantasy I have about owning a sex slave?"

Her eyes opened slumberously and she smiled. "No. But I think I'd like for you to tell me about it right now."

He showed her instead.

It's hot...
and it's out of control!

It's a two-alarm Blaze—
from one of Temptation's newest authors!

This spring, Temptation turns up the heat. Look
for these bold, provocative, *ultra*-sexy books!

#679 PRIVATE PLEASURES
Janelle Denison
April 1998

Mariah Stevens wanted a husband. Grey Nichols
wanted a lover. But Mariah was determined.
For better or worse, there would be no more private
pleasures for Grey without a public ceremony.

#682 PRIVATE FANTASIES
Janelle Denison
May 1998

For Jade Stevens, Kyle was the man of her dreams. He
seemed to know her every desire—in bed and out. Little
did she know that he'd come across her book of private
fantasies—or that he intended to make every one come true!

BLAZE! Red-hot reads from Temptation!

HARLEQUIN®
Temptation

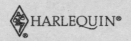

Not The Same Old Story!

 Exciting, glamorous romance stories that take readers around the world.

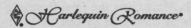 Sparkling, fresh and tender love stories that bring you pure romance.

 Bold and adventurous— Temptation is strong women, bad boys, great sex!

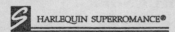 Provocative and realistic stories that celebrate life and love.

 Contemporary fairy tales—where anything is possible and where dreams come true.

 Heart-stopping, suspenseful adventures that combine the best of romance and mystery.

L͟OVE & L͟AUGHTER Humorous and romantic stories that capture the lighter side of love.

THE MEN OF BACHELOR CREEK

Alaska. A place where men could be men—and women were scarce!

To Tanner, Joe and Hawk, Alaska was the final frontier. They'd gone to the ends of the earth to flee the one thing they all feared—MATRIMONY. Little did they know that three intrepid heroines would brave the wilds to "save" them from their lonely bachelor existences.

Enjoy

**#662 CAUGHT UNDER
THE MISTLETOE!
December 1997**

**#670 DODGING CUPID'S ARROW!
February 1998**

**#678 STRUCK BY SPRING FEVER!
April 1998**

by Kate Hoffmann

Available wherever Harlequin books are sold.

**Look for these titles—
available at your favorite retail outlet!**

January 1998
Renegade Son by Lisa Jackson
Danielle Summers had problems: a rebellious child.
and unscrupulous enemies. In addition, her Montana
ranch was slowly being sabotaged. And then there was
Chase McEnroe—who admired her land and desired her
body. But Danielle feared he would invade more than just
her property—he'd trespass on her heart.

February 1998
The Heart's Yearning by Ginna Gray
Fourteen years ago Laura gave her baby up for adoption,
and not one day had passed that she didn't think about
him and agonize over her choice—so she finally followed
her heart to Texas to see her child. But the plan to watch
her son from afar doesn't quite happen that way, once the
boy's sexy—*single*—father takes a decided interest in *her*.

March 1998
First Things Last by Dixie Browning
One look into Chandler Harrington's dark eyes and
Belinda Massey could refuse the Virginia millionaire nothing.
So how could the no-nonsense nanny believe the rumors that
he had kidnapped his nephew—an adorable, healthy little boy
who crawled as easily into her heart as he did into her lap?

**BORN IN THE USA: Love, marriage—
and the pursuit of family!**

Look us up on-line at: http://www.romance.net

BUSA4

HARLEQUIN®

Temptation

It's a dating wasteland out there! So what's a girl to do when there's not a marriage-minded man in sight? Go hunting, of course.

Manhunting

Enjoy the hilarious antics of five intrepid heroines, determined to lead Mr. Right to the altar—whether he wants to go or not!

#669 *Manhunting in Memphis—*
Heather MacAllister (February 1998)

#673 *Manhunting in Manhattan—*
Carolyn Andrews (March 1998)

#677 *Manhunting in Montana—*
Vicki Lewis Thompson (April 1998)

#681 *Manhunting in Miami—*
Alyssa Dean (May 1998)

#685 *Manhunting in Mississippi—*
Stephanie Bond (June 1998)

She's got a plan—to find herself a man!

Available wherever Harlequin books are sold.